Rumi's Daughter

Meral Alizada

ISBN: 978-1-5272-8322-0

Table of Contents

Author's Note

To the heart who has given me the chance to be a part of your hands and your bookshelf, I thank you.

It was written for you to be holding these pages and to begin the journey you are yet to embark upon.

I hope that you find a quiet, beloved place to begin the narration of a little girl's transition from childhood to adulthood, seeking the very thing that you seek in all you pursue, peace.

Rumi's Daughter is a collection of poems written in blood and breath, for those hearts who find themselves worn thin in a world such as ours.

When I began life, I could see quite clearly, a people in dire need of healing. I could see how hard we go, how far we will cross to reach the thing that makes us feel utterly and completely safe.

As a child bent on an innate inclination towards love, I saw, as you have, the forms of love that we chase and in tasting every one, my tongue knew quite clearly both their beauties and their lethal potentials.

I have seen far too many beautiful souls taken out by the world, punished and reduced.

I decided for it to be my life's purpose to find the secret that would take us above our pain and incompleteness. It was a naive, idealist belief but one that I never gave up on.

Having completed 300 so poems in lockdown, I contemplated over the right name to give the book. Rumi, I discovered after I began to write my poetry, and my aunt pointed to the similar essence and message of our bodies work. There cannot be another Rumi and I for one, certainly cannot be, but Rumi has touched the lives of those who hold religion and do not, from the West and the East, his work has cut across borders because of the simple humanness of his message. With the same breath, I welcome you with the same blindness to yourself. From whichever path, from whichever place, these pages welcome you with wide and open arms. There is a place in this book that will speak to you, that yearns to hold and embrace you.

Rumi's Daughter seeks but one purpose, to pave the way for soul relief, the birth right of every man, woman and child.

If we are to look beyond the harsh tongues, the distancing and even cruelty, we see a deep need for liberation that cannot come from any part of the external world.

From every page turn, I wish from every part of my heart, strength and silence to find a way towards the eye of the mountain top so that you can see the entire plain of yourself.

In our journey together, we are coming back, for every day that was in pain, for every smile that could have been, and yet was not.

We are coming back to fill each passed moment with its rightful bliss. We are coming to take back, every bit of you that you long to hold again.

It is my promise that you will regain all that you lost in this place. And there will be a gain far more than what you first set out to pursue.

My words are a mere beginning, you are the beautiful and final end.

In love and light,

Meral

Instagram: @MeralPoetess
Website: MeralAlizada.com

Acknowledgements

In the Remembrance of Allah Subhanahu wa Ta'ala, Allah e Paak, Allah e Aziz, I am tongue-tied in my loving of You, You hold full and entire credit to every word written. My entire journey was orchestrated by You, You moved my heart and Determined for me to follow Your Path, I am both mind and soul alive only because of You.

To my late grandfather and grandmother who stood for kindness, for mercy and unconditional loving until their last breath, I hope to carry the legacy you both began. Rest in eternal peace.

To my beloved Curly, you were the first face this face saw after the battle was through. Your face and forgiveness, induced a love and hope for people and life again. You are gentleness, sincerity, kindness and whole truth living, but even these words are unable to capture you. You who scatters charity and selflessness in his path, who taught me tenderness, humanness, integrity and self honouring again. You brought back to me, myself. I will never be rid of the love I have of you, entire chambers and worlds in my heart are dedicated to you. He Brought you to me, so that I may learn from you, what it means to believe in Him.

To Kozsheen, my beloved sister and woman of noor, you turned my face towards the face of Islam I now know. The Shams to my Rumi, I am a mere extension of the philosophy you imbued onto me.

To my sister, Ghuzal, who looks towards her life with a treasure chest of potential, I pray these words can come to surround and remain faithful to you as you begin to make your way into the world.

To the world, and to the oppressor who catapulted all of this into fruition, I forgive you.

To all of you, I love you, I thank you, for your love, your support, the welcome arms with which you received me, an unknown pained poet. You gave me the strength to put the most concealed parts of myself to paper.

I would like to note that this book is not for the sake of self promotion or to further my name, but to further The Name of God, The Name of the Merciful and Kind Creator Whose Path I have given my personal narration to. This is not an attempt to convert, change minds but to leave the door open to Contemplation and a universal chance to find the essence of the most intricate secret of existence.

My path led me to knowing the truth of this life and to move for the sake of Him and Him alone. I am removed from this book, He is Eternally Present and with you at each page turn.

Cover Art: Farangiz Masumova Instagram: **@De_overthinkers**
Illustrations: Samea Shanori Instagram: **@Samea.Shanori.art**

Section One: The Centre

We begin from here
We are born from The Centre
The compound build-up of the foundation
From which we leap into the world
The eyes and arms and heart through which the rest of the world,
Becomes.
The thread line that weaves itself so intimately
Into the hems and shoulder lines of our beings
That our seeds are planted from this place
And we will enter this place again and again
We begin at The Centre
And we remember the first foot towards
The Horizon
The point of time,
That the rest of life
Points back towards and into.
We begin at the beginning.
We begin at The Centre.

I am dreaming,

I am dreaming of an open home

And kind words

I am dreaming of having

Come from love, too

I dream that I do not find myself

In suffocation upon waking

I dream of pinewood roast

And food made with love

And I am dreaming…

I am dreaming of waking to the quiet

I am dreaming of soft skin and curls

And gentleness made in softened fire.

I am dreaming of waking with lightness

I dream of being set free of,

Released

Of this boulder upon my chest

I am dreaming of home,

I am dreaming of little,

And to me,

This is the gaining of the world entire.

Meral Alizada

The absence of something,
Felt right from the
Beginning of memory.
All these dreams emit longing
To reach some destination,
And never getting there.
In search,
In wonderment and exile
Longing to hold onto something
That would keep the soul alive
In the terrifying awareness
Of the fragility of life
And the pace of time,
And its running out too
These eyes searched into oceans
Across celestial orbs
And in the eye of each path companion
For its settling place
For the salvation of the soul,
And found none

Meral Alizada

The nights spent convincing
This child heart to put itself together
That cracks and splinters
In the rise of the sun,
Arriving into irreconcilable pieces
By dusk

Meral Alizada

A thousand voices,

A thousand vices

Their starved eyes

That run their dirty hands

And their unclean minds

Over this marble slab canvas

That within had all it contained

Required not removal and replacement

But restoration,

Embrace

A reservation for His Place

For surely,

There can be no error in His Making

Meral Alizada

Who will take me from
This place?
Where neither logic
Reconciliation,
Nor Civil peace
Knows no recognition,
Nor face.

Meral Alizada

We children,

Spectrums of different light

Walking with a thousand colours

To be painted black

And grayscale

In entry to our confinement

We are but an extension of him.

Our shoulders hold up

His lies

And we pull the carts of this smoken imposterity

His puppeteers,

His strings, our limbs

A duressed promise of obedience

To him,

Comes the certainty of

Lifelong betrayal to ourselves.

Meral Alizada

Freak show

Hybrid

Shadow,

Beach footprint of the self

Narrowed down

Shaved inwards

Cut and pulled,

Moulded and smothered

Facade built over

The gravestone of the self

Buried alive

But still moving

Daily hammer in

Obliteration of any sign of life

And yet it screams,

It cannot be forgotten.

The thing, it aches

To be known

To be given a chance

Just one chance,

To be seen.

Is there no trace of value within me

That I must emulate anything,

Anyone,

But myself?

Meral Alizada

I lived this childhood
Vicariously
Through their laughter
The sounds of which, have
Never rolled on our tongues
Handing over everything we hold,
To the first and only bidder.

Meral Alizada

Chameleon

To be ourselves,
Was not enough
Chameleon,
You bend and break
And fall and rise
And contort and twist
For once upon a time,
Over several years,
You were put out in the cold,
Made to feel ashamed of
The very skin that covers you.

Meral Alizada

You hold no place in our lives.

Without you,

We would only know peace.

What and who are you to command?

Who gave you this place?

The whip for fulfilling the

Commandments you do not touch.

Hypocrite

You cannot contain yourself,

So you contain us.

Meral Alizada

We kid ourselves of what we want

Our desires,

Advance prescriptions

We have no say.

For the access to the inner voice

Is kept from us

And we are carcasses

In school clothes

Knowing burden before

If ever, having known play

Meral Alizada

Do not ask me who I am

I, a life long subject

Operation and modification

Of a mind, body

And soul

That needed neither

That came as Allah intended

To whom to place even a shadow

Of a hand that itches to modify,

An unforgivable crime.

I am bludgeoned

Canister gas lit into believing

Is an act of mercy

Meral Alizada

My skin crawls in protest

This is not my world,
This is not my place.
In the stench of *kuhul,*
The breath of zam-zam
Lingers
I flee
Finding a place in this cold shack,
A place its *zam* does not chlorinate
You mix our home with sweat
You dampen
And drown what has begun to swim
And your wrongdoings,
It casts upon her rounded face,
An imprint she did not bring upon herself
No wonder we all choke
No wonder, all we do is choke.

Meral Alizada

Sickening

My sweetness, is sickening

A goodness without a cause

Feet blistered for each walk towards righteousness

Surrounded by the place that demands anything but

What use of this is there?

What use is there of this, in here?

Meral Alizada

Death to the Messenger

No truth of the self within
But eyes,
Eyes to see the greater truth
Amongst the self blinded
This was not only death,
For death was once and complete.
This was a death that died more and more,
With each passing day.

Meral Alizada

I count the steps
In between the lashings
And I count the fingers on my hand
As they sometimes do
When they sit on the velvet mat
In every moment of quiet
I pour out
You are known to be in the skies
And there is a garden party to the left
And our hell in the middle
Three hearts in rhythms of slow beat
If this is punishment,
Give her punishment to me.

Meral Alizada

As you chalk out
Our existence
And ready the hound dogs
And bulls to chow down
Our diversions
Into your cardboard cut out,
I look up beyond this secret prison,
And the clouds they take centre stage,
From their height, they speak,
That there surely must be some authority
Further and mightier than you.
That can lead the way upwards
For this kind of containment,
Could not be the only place,
That we can ever aspire to come to.

Meral Alizada

There is no place

For this gentleness within

That wishes to spread

That whispers,

Enquiring of her release

And I push her face back into the lighthouse

Of the voice box

And we await

For the field

With a soil,

That can receive and grow these seeds of the tenderness of a voice,

That dare not be spoken here.

Meral Alizada

We do not do wrong
She does no wrong
Her head is hung in duty
And mine in subservience,
Yet why do You give to others in wholes,
What we have not held in fractions?

Meral Alizada

Cursed are we,

Birthed into burden

From the plain of the Unwanted,

We hurl ourselves against these walls

Our cuts so determined,

So that we take up no more of the expanding space,

We already occupy

Meral Alizada

The heart will always seek its owner,

The child will always call for mother

But for those who may never know of a home

Become masterminds

Genius and unloved,

The Van Goghs

And Monets,

Painting out worlds for ourselves

Plays across every stage of imagination's dimensions

Home known in the most unconnected of things.

Meral Alizada

Different sides of the spectrum

Victimisation

Hereditary exploitation

From this cruelty

I was born

And they wonder

They ask why I run electric

Child never at ease

Caught in the mind

A daily self reconciliation

After self hatred

Hopeless and helpless

And sometimes nothing to piece together, again

I am the *product* of this

Meral Alizada

I murder the foul of my blood
I strengthen the child of the meek
And go to war with the child of the tyrant
Too much power
Too little power,
How do we reconcile
The irreconcilable?

Meral Alizada

When each day begins with battle

And ends with bloody defeat,

And we walk on to find no fruit in its end

And this battle is neither lost nor won,

But continues through,

A war spanning my entire lifetime.

There can be no end to this

When the foundation,

Is so without a foundation

Meral Alizada

We leave the womb

Running

Spinning,

And jumping

Lifelong performers

Circus

The silence

Such intimate acquaintance with misery

And its homed capture in our beings

Meral Alizada

We could not conquer
The four walls
We were raised within
How can we walk forth
In hope of the acceptance
We could not even know here?

Meral Alizada

I sit before you two,

And I wonder

How could she,

Love's love

Ever come to knock at my door

For I am made

From two souls

Who in a thousand worlds

Would not choose each other

Who would not seek to mingle a shared word,

With each other.

Meral Alizada

What must we have done,

In some other life

Murder, pillage, rape?

To deserve one as reckless as this?

Our compass,

Broken

How can we know direction?

Meral Alizada

Qurbani

I tap
Purple buds fall out
Against my fingertips
I have traded all of the rest of my breaths
And the rest of my beats
In return of your rescue
Topple Genghis' fort
Her livelihood
At the butchers' knife
The sound of knives sharpening
The struggle of the lamb
And then,
Then!
The modest blood spills
Protecting its predator
Even when the sacrifice is through
And us bouncing and throwing against the picket fences,
Eyes blood cup
Turned, whimper at the window
The window that never,
Not once,
Spoke.

Meral Alizada

I would give up this pen
And this strange,
Unyielding tolerance
So out of place
In this infant body
For the sake of living one day in the skin of
The smiling blonde girl
How it would feel to hold her swaying lunchbox
So happy to go home
How can you be
So happy to go
Home?

Meral Alizada

And yet in the heart of that storm,

There remained a sanctuary

An inner sanctuary

And I ran from place to place, trying to find a place

To listen to

To breathe in,

To hold all noises at the gates

So that this voice may have its slot and be

Heard in its solitary spotlight

Full amplification

Meral Alizada

The skies are embracing
The moon, mother, father, sister.
The waves and the silence
Forehead kisses, hair caress.
Gorging on make belief
Gorging on all that comes close
A grip so tight,
Knuckles so white,
That water draws poison
And friendship runs to enmity

Meral Alizada

Docklands

We are docklands.
Watchtowers,
The sirens on the boulders
And the satellite receptors
We are stationed everywhere,
We are searching in anywhere,
Determined to hold again,
What was taken from the cradle.

Meral Alizada

Running,

Shielding

From them,

The little heart

That loves beauty

Adores the clean

And the silence

I run with the child of the chest

And find sleep in the wilderness

This is my city and civilisation

Meral Alizada

The Peace Cavern

I cower into the corner,
Retreated into my indulgence,
For those prized
Beloved moments of rest
Of earned breath,
The books spread
The innocence of blank paper
The clean place
Of which only good enters
And only good leaves
And my heart smiles,
If only once.
In so long
But it smiles,
Yes, it smiles,
For it is given what it is.

Meral Alizada

I know a face
Within this face,
That shows its face
Even in that brutality
I can somehow disarmour
At the green gates of eight am,
And I can enter the hideout
Of crayons, scoopballs and nets
And their eyes light,
The joy of filling the spaces beside me

Meral Alizada

I am seeking the place

That has sent for me,

So many invitations

Beyond the smoke and dust,

Let me see!

What is being kept from me?

What is across the bridge from me?

Let me see!

Yet I am terrified that if it cannot be found,

There is deception awaiting at the foot of the bridge

Of what

And of whom will I become,

Without an answer?

Meral Alizada

A Great Triumph

Why this feeling?
Why such baseless comforting?
That this hope,
Can and will,
Someday
Somehow,
Become saving.
Will all of this be for some reason?
And move us close to that closeness?
Will there be…
It feels as if, somehow, it will be.
Could there be...
As if all of this
Without giving itself away as to when,
Will one day,
One shining day,
Come to great triumph

Meral Alizada

Cliff Throws

Our determinants
Broke our hearts
Before anyone else stood
A chance
And all that followed
Was free fall,
From the first
Of several thousand cliff throws

Meral Alizada

My face is turned,
So busy protecting you
And your livelihood,
And yet gaining your love
Is in the broom sweep
And the scrub of floors,
For the child who struggles with
Her buttons,
And her laces forever undone,
I work for your admiration
For your embrace,
That in what I do with my books
And my voice and learning,
Can gain me the love,
You give to them.

Meral Alizada

I will know of a love

That makes the sparkle eye

Of Paris jealous

That sits with comfort

And ease

With flow between

Menu and sunshine

I will know of the tasting of truth

And nothing but the truth,

In our shining pools

A truth that is easy

Rawness that requires no peeling

But unravels,

Without effort of request

Meral Alizada

The voice of child song

Broken into

By the heartbreak thud of the oppressors

Swallowed into the apple of Adam,

I wonder if this voice will always

Hold song in its voice box,

I wonder if this mind will remember

The eyelids

Will they retain the light of the sun

They once touched?

In this underground prison sentence,

And in the barren walls of these caves

Will they remember?

Will there be song

Retained in my memory?

Will my voice still hold

The box of the child song?

Meral Alizada

Adieu

The shoulders you burdened on me
I have no attachment,
Nor dependency
No tear to shed,
And no ache for a smile to hold me either.
The child born fully grown
The child heart will give me energy
The adult eyes
Will seek what is being sought
And all the bones in between
Will hold up this voyage,
And I will find my tribe
I will know what it is
They knew
But for now,
To the days of the playground
To the races across the mounded hill,
To that world,
We bid
But I don't want to,
We bid,
Must I need to?

A d i e u

Meral Alizada

In the cold corners

The silence of this neglect,

The colourlessness of home's canvas,

A drop of colour permeates the wall

Minuscule

But enough for me to believe,

There is some rose

Of cashmere colour

To be seeded

Meral Alizada

I have memorised

Every note of the melodies of

Morning bird song

Not an inch, unknown.

No note of the morning scent that I have not gushed

Into my throat

Not an inch left

For discovery in the snowflakes that fall anew each time

So what does one do,

When the morning mist and branches,

The berries and rustled leaves

Are gnashed and stomached

And you sign,

Hungry,

But my child,

There is nothing that can fill you here.

Meral Alizada

I took refuge in the water
And in the books
In never worlds,
And what could never be.
They attacked
And they exhumed their exhausts
Asphyxiated, but breath breathes warm.
We somehow survived,
As if we were meant to.

Meral Alizada

The formed masculine soul,

Brooding

Baby face in

Lancelot's armour,

Of its first, and shining new

The eyes set burning at the horizon

All compasses turned heavenwards,

And all eyes of the crew stapled at sea level

Meral Alizada

Little me, she stands at the shore

And I turned

From the harbour

The anchor reeled in

The sails of the ship howling,

Yet drowned, drizzled down

By the sound of her gaze,

Those heavy waiting eyes

In a thing meant to thrive in not knowing

And when I turned,

I promised

And I left the most tender part of her with me

And she stood in her overalls

And

Those eyes,

Saucer sized

Smiling in her faith of me

Moving not a single inch,

In promise of the tomorrow liberation

And for those lips,

And for the dimpled smile,

Does this ship set sail

And do the shoulders brood and buckle

For that unmoving loyalty

For the little heart

That believed and gave so much love,

Her moon gaze that holds

Between the waves and us.

This ship sails

Steadied and weathering these storms,

Of your milken breath,

Fortune will come to accompany

Meral Alizada

Open space

And wind breeze skin

A life of sincerity

The widening of a world

Far extended from the four corners

Of this cardboard box

I will make that dent,

I will make that change

I will claim all birthrights

What I could not find from here,

Please, let it be found

Over there.

Meral Alizada

Section Two: The Reach

When the home does not warm the hands,
The cold pushes us out into the bleakness of the world
So we reach at any flame, to thaw our blue and purple tips.

Meral Alizada

Open palms

A giving spring that keeps giving,

And smiling arms that shoulder the world,

How lovely is this face,

How lovelier will it become?

    - I will love the world and it will love me too

Meral Alizada

All the love left over,
All the love incarcerated,
It gushes from my eyes
There is so much love,
And so great and wide of a world
To hand all of myself over to

Meral Alizada

A Promise to the Heart

In self embrace,
The skies they weep with me
In my silent loneliness,
I began to speak
A letter to the self
Consolation to the moon high heart,
Dearest one,
In some other life,
With some other pot of luck,
The grandeur and pure of your heart will be found
And held much earlier on
You will know health of bond
Comfort and trust
As was written in those beloved books of yours
You will know surety from the love you give,
So that you may leave this world
As a woman who loved,
And was miraculously,
Wholeheartedly,
And absolutely,
Loved back.

Meral Alizada

And so you would spend a lifetime
Taking from your mountain
Handing out these gold bars
Knowing you would come to dust,
For the sake of some pitiful
Fair weather company

Meral Alizada

The nightly positioning

The teeth chewed

The grinding of the wagons towards that place

Set out for,

But never reached

The stealth neck

Craned upwards

Towards the sky,

The murmurs and the moving,

And the arms outstretched,

Yearning to be held.

Meral Alizada

I watch you,

As a stranger would

I notice you,

As a bypasser would

You walk around and you

Illuminate and peel out the faint traces

Of goodness in people,

And leave them a little better

And leave yourself, a little worse

Meral Alizada

There is no other choice

But to hold

And keep to hope

When all is lost

For there was nothing to begin with,

All may be lost, but the ray of hope itself

And to her we keep

And to the skies, we keep watch

Meral Alizada

The reach upwards
The daily and nightly
Longing
The star gazing
And love's shape forming
I trace its neckline
Imprint the scent of its flesh,
The tender of its neck
This is how it'll be
This is how he will *certainly*,
Be.

Meral Alizada

How she could make the most deserted of human beings, oceanic.
Sculpting the ordinary into beacons of perfection.
Making anyone, and everyone, lovable and so loved.
For the love she gave, was a reflection of her.
Her desperate need to paint the world of reality into the world of her
dreams.
So she took those darkened souls and forgave and forgot their sins.
Giving birth a thousand times a day.
Just to cope.
Just to continue.
And what better way than to reimagine the world as you dream it.
Looking at the face of your love, and loving not who they are, but
Who they are after your fairytales have laid their hand on them.

Meral Alizada

You love the world

Your eyes sparkle

At the sight of a new way of living

Your chest fills with delight

As you hear the tongue of a faraway land

You are deeply

In love with people

And while you love,

You swallow the hope that

They could in turn,

Love you

Meral Alizada

The starvation of love

Saw me ripping open my heart

And seeing the entirety of it

Astounded and mesmerised at each part of it

Able to see it in the smallest cracks of any smile

And any smile

Can become affection

And any warmth,

The face of love

Meral Alizada

When the beating in the home

Becomes so severe,

Every stranger sentiment feels like pilgrimage

Meral Alizada

Their happiness, my happiness
Their joy,
Felt within me too
A laughter erupts
And I find myself
Singing along
In its exact tune
A perfect recreation
Of its melody

Meral Alizada

You've been kept at such distances,
That you've made loving from afar,
A beautiful kind of existence

Meral Alizada

I am an addict

I am an addict,
High from the sight of love
Its most loyal journalist
Its most artful
Mind photographer
Stomach filled from its smell and its after drops from several thousand
Miles away.
I bathe in the aroma left of two lovers in their exchange.
I feel it within the earth.
The transience of warm yellow pain pulled between two people.
Who walked not on Earth, but some other place known by the few.
The very lucky few.

Meral Alizada

My negotiations

For love

Eloquence of argument

Compelling,

Compelling reasons

You pitched perfectly

But handed no investment

The pitiful bargaining for a place

In their hearts

You moved to silver and shine rise high

Needle in the hay

This kind of devotion

Oversaturated

No place for a devotion

As this

What do you devote yourself to?

The pens

And paper

Blood stench

The machine grinds

No allies here

Fill the desk

And keep the chest hollow

This was not your territory

And your heavy chest of potential

There was no place

For the likes of you in this chamber of luxuries

No place for you here,

And no place for you there.

Meral Alizada

This was how it was, always.

My passionate turns your way

And the lukewarm indifference of yours.

Brief

Reciprocated by remembrance of duty.

Returned, never initiated.

Meral Alizada

You've performed in the tightest of viewing spaces

That you are a chameleon,

Who looks

To the heart

Of the object of desire

Channels

Whispers,

And like magic,

Transforms

And echoes

Out

Vibrations

That meet exactly with theirs

Meral Alizada

I wake to the song of your longing

You are the purpose of it all

The essence of my being

The reason my steps hit the ground so furiously

Because the streets have become love

And the lights, its continuum

Meral Alizada

Everything that you are from,

Everything that your world is of

The fact of your existence

Breaks me into twirls into the hours of the midnight

The heaven,

And the hell

I want it all

If it means holding the warmth of your hand for a lifetime.

Meral Alizada

I will love you before you have entered the room and shatter with the
Weight of this feeling when you leave
I will fall deeply in love with the rays that find ways into your eyes
My soul forlorn at the waking newness of desire for you
I will circle and magnify my heart to yours in the faint traces of
Your goodness
Every act of yours, a miracle
Every smile of yours, saviour
I have found ways of loving strangers in new ways, again and again
And yet in all this time,
All this love for humanity,
I could not find it within me,
To love me

Meral Alizada

It was love I said

She asked, *how did you know?*

When he laughed

And it rippled

Through my veins

And forced both my mind

And heart

To collapse in on itself

Meral Alizada

You were to me,

As moonlight is to the face of the sea

Meral Alizada

Why do they all leap ten feet...

From which place can I find these tools

With which to mend myself?

What must I lessen?

Will my dismembering

Mellow this revolt?

Meral Alizada

Little louder gesture of self proclamation

A higher pitched laugh

More warmth in gaze

More and more

For it is not enough

The audience craves more

Give us more!

And at the velvet drop

My own hands

Latch onto my throat

This soul would not allow it

A life of puritan spirit

In a world that did not tire from excrement

Meral Alizada

This noise and these ruined dreams

Their villainy

That clogs clarified waters

And myself, refusing to mix

So I have sat as oil at the bottom of water

Refusing to mingle

Slow torture for my refusal

I cannot intermingle

I cannot become of this,

The penance for incapacity,

Paid in lifelong blood

Meral Alizada

There have been many a shows

Many feasts and dances

That I have stood and watched

From afar,

The heaviness of the air

It carried and cocooned their voices

And I sat at the foot of nature's beckoning

The sound of crickets

And the transition of the skies

Warming my heart to distract

From the coldness of theirs

Meral Alizada

Useful,

An open treasure chest of benefit

She approached the world

With her CV written across her face,

Her shoulders and arms

Knowing only one thing

That if you love hard enough,

If you learn to destroy yourself keenly enough,

You might, just might be qualified

For half hearted

Affection

Sheep skin

Wolf

The hyenas that wear the mask of

Such convincing affection

Meral Alizada

Let Me In

This world
That celebrates the coquettish
The charm
But not simpleness
I am a person of truth
I have been beating at doors,
I bring goodness
Let me in
These eyes they know no motive,
But these eyes party to your life do
Let me in,
My place is not out in the cold
My place is amongst you

Meral Alizada

Why do they reject me
But take what I can give to them
Why will they have what I feed
But the feeder stands outback
Why does this world only ransack
Only take from me
More and more of me
Without the cost of having me

Meral Alizada

Silenced, was the time kill and shamanism

You told me

In this way,

Do not look so forlorn

At their leaping and froing

The shrill and shriek of their voices

This may be the height of what they will see

And only a glimpse of what you will be

Those hands that fold in elegant openness

Your walk and face invites not glare

But intrigued awareness

They see you,

They know your place

It is known to everyone,

But you

Meral Alizada

I came to celebrate the end of the white collar t shirts

A dream of some relief killed yet again

By the same killers

In mother's land

Smiling for the sake of their smiling

My lifeforce yet again, depleting

And from the corner of the eye,

A dusten green and gold

A Quran

In this place of all places?

Amongst those to whom bread share

Is such stock loss,

I looked upon it once

And the heart moved to look again,

As the face you see once

And come to find them years again

And they strike you as if you will know them better

At some point,

But perhaps not now.

As if I would come to know this face sincerely

And in full

But as if some jewels were to be acquired

Before this would be

Before this privilege

Would come to be held in full grasp

In *my* hands

Meral Alizada

I saw your face and asked not

But a finger from you,

Only that you stay

So that I may give the first breath of a love

That is not yet touched by the world

The love that knew not the knowledge of heartbreak

And yet you ran.

And beyond the running,

You chose for a lust

That spat and chewed

Yellow urination on the snow white canvas

I preserved for you.

Meral Alizada

Had you asked for the moon,
I would have found a way,
By God, I would have found a way

Meral Alizada

I have been fascinated by all

But never the subject of fascination

Loved all

Without condition

And only loved,

Upon condition

So do not ask me

To be feminine

To be delicate,

Restrained,

Prim and proper

You tampered with an innocent soul

No choice but to rip from myself

To be masculine and jagged,

All sharp knives and toxic fume

To be heavy and deliberate

Awaiting the turn of the corner.

I came to be this way,

No one was born hardened.

Meral Alizada

And when the heart breaks, the skies become the healer, blanket wrap.
And the moon, the confidant, a sturdy shoulder.

Meral Alizada

The suffocation was what I feared the most
Learning more with every day how to live
Without the person you swore,
Was at the book corners of your lifeline

Meral Alizada

I have failed perhaps because love

And my hands do not hold.

And thus, I can only come to know release.

My daughter will come to know peace.

And her daughter, respect.

Her daughter, love.

And her daughter,

Perhaps *her* daughter, will know

God.

Meral Alizada

Perhaps not in this lifetime

But the next,

You will not find yourself

Tilting to meet the rise and stunt

Of each axis

You will not find yourself lost in the wave

Of your own pains

Watching the world taste a comfort

Unbeknownst to you

You will not need to run

From person to person,

Proving, performing,

Rising and falling

You will not hurt so,

For what is the damned state of

Luck in this lifetime,

May be the seed of reward,

For the next..

Meral Alizada

I could not have done more for you,

Yet I could not do the tenderness

That entices you

And for your heart,

My bones worked thin

And your love for the women

Who do not cast an eyelash your way

But give themselves

All of themselves

And somehow,

This is the little that is needed

To fill you.

Meral Alizada

I wanted nothing more than

Someone who looks to me

With simple tenderness

And gentle eyes

Who holds me

As glass is held

And leather worn

Who forgives my tongue

And sees in me,

What my own blood

Cannot see in me

Who anchors me

Shelters me,

Whose kindness,

Gives a chance to me

Meral Alizada

In less than a heartbeat,

I would trade all of this cleverness,

For magnetism

Meral Alizada

I've noticed love through
The ruffled curtains of
Warm winter houses
Read of its glory
In mahsanavis and folktales
Of the Orient
In the secret glances
Of street couples
And in the steady hands
Of children of peace-homes
It has remained close,
But I have not held it.
Yet many of its imposters
Having promised its name
And delivering none,
Have come and sipped on
My lifeline
And rendered me incapable
Of deciphering
Foam from fog
O Love, if you come,
I have little to give you
I have nothing to give you

Meral Alizada

My first friend in this new world

I did not take up another

We stood side by side

Our hands stayed touched

But it was only my hand that clutched yours

I did not move an inch further

Without pushing you forward

And you took off

Superhuman speed

The moment you understood the reigns

You accelerated

And I,

I removed my foot altogether

Meral Alizada

I knew then when

I turned into the street,

My eyes yearning to see

The final rites of

Two years of sisterhood

Her eyes on the mattress

My eyes memorising the last of her

The first friend in this place

Never a friend

From the beginning and always a sister,

Engine of the car

The first time we got lost on campus,

The first time we looked at a case

The slow move off

Into the road,

The last I saw of her,

My heart in my hands,

Whimpering

Demanding of me to know,

How it could be that the human heart

Could move fast along

Such elegant amnesia

Heartbreak in friendship

Kills in ways,

Love of romance

Is incapable of

Meral Alizada

Do not ask me to take deep breaths

When my lungs choke from the

Weight of the smoke within

Do not ask me to be delicate

The world took from me,

My balance long ago

Do not ask me to be calm

For I can no longer think

Do not ask me to be hopeful

For we took from the earth,

All that is worth the ignition of hope

Do not ask me to stand down

My guard to open and receive

That leads to the alleyways

To desert lands,

The fringes of society

A one-way road to exploitation

Do not ask me to give

For I woke with a burning hope

Every morning

And gave its warmth

To everything that moved

Put out,

I don't have it in me

Anymore

Meral Alizada

There is a limit

Even upon the expanding fluidity of the human heart

A fountain stop on the generosity of the soul

When the good is beaten into

And laid in deepening wounds

Sores and bubonic plague

When the capacity for tolerance,

When the principles for goodness

Begin to loosen

The giving

The forever giving,

Begins to show its receipts

And loyalty,

Discovers the option

Of disloyalty

But I,

I reached not for the gun to wound others,

But myself

Petal by petal,

The beast's rose

Began to droop

And slowly,

The skin begins to crack

The water sits in hair,

T Shirt

Slowly the hoarding

And so little of it used

The shame of self loving

The fear in self care,

Little by little,

The plain face that emerges

And the wrists feather light

Without its bracelets

The cobwebbed earlobes

The weight of its matching earrings

Felt and yet not so,

Slowly,

Their wishes for my downfall came true,

When Russian Roulette sat in the place

Of cleanser, toner, moisturiser

Massage.

Meral Alizada

The oppressed turn against the world
I could not,
So I turned against myself

Meral Alizada

There are several deaths we face in one lifetime

Before the final and ultimate passing

But none more devastating

Than the death of innocence

And the birth of the vice

That becomes of the heartbroken child

That gave good until it no longer could.

Meral Alizada

Section Three: The Defeat

I came to that city
Laced with hope
The urgency of the fairytale
Glazed over my eyes
Shot out like missile calls
Come in,
Come in
Target located
Begin the war cry
No village must remain
This place will flatten
Zion built over the bones
And stretched over the flesh
Of Haifa
Boomed out
The hawk hollows
The fetish for detonation
So resden and orange vivid
I set myself ablaze
My life had burned at the stake
And so I must lose even more
Than what was first lost

Meral Alizada

All I had, had been taken

And so I descended into

Sodom and Gommorah

With nothing but myself to set fire to

For I had left that face

And all that it was associated with

The death of that sisterhood

And the killing of first love

How could have betrayal come

From two who look

As birds do?

And I came

With my heart cut open

The shamed stench

Of my defeat

The corridors sunk heavy

And I called out

In every way that I could

Those clean walls

Shiny little room

It smells as morgues do

And so

Decaying flesh

And the white flag surrender

Drew the vultures

And the wolves close

The hyenas they cackled

The tenderness of that ruin

Salivation of those vampires

It was as if it walked ahead of me

As if I were paralysed

From commanding it otherwise

So consumed,

Overcome

As I had gone so far

That this had become my place

I had danced with these devils,

Was it only time

That I became one too?

Meral Alizada

From the mirror I trace her new face,

Nostalgia.

I miss her white eyes

And her self-contained happiness

I miss her conviction,

The emblem of her proud sobriety

I miss her innocence

I miss her exhausting imagination

But above all,

I miss her utmost belief in

The good heart of people

Meral Alizada

You cast me to the wolves
Took what was raw from me,
I will never hold the love
I had for you
In my hands again,
You cast me from the sanctuary
The home I built for you
And in the streets, they found me
In the gutter, they raise me.

Meral Alizada

A schoolgirl's death

Flame fire

And fire

And flame,

I tossed her into the middle

Of that world of packed lunches

Casio watch

I threw her

Limbs and all

Screaming

School tie's death

Those clothes

Were never to be worn again

That face,

Never to be known

That heart, never to beat in rhythm again.

Meral Alizada

It broke me
As grief breaks
A further manifestation
Into a greater monster
One that would be with me
For years
That would sit in the lining
Of every moment that could hold
Some promise of happiness
That would rise in the throat
Of each gesture of sincerity
A world of chaos
And illogical assumption
A new fetish for one's own
Toppling,
A new love for past pain,
And a suspicion of the calm
An ease with shadow sitting
And a hatred for new light

Meral Alizada

My heart belongs to some distant land,

Some direction into the Orient

Where the clothes are heavy in embroidery

And the hearts light in prayer

Where the moon and the sun

Rise and *rukoh*

In perfect punctuality of sajdah

And so why am I dressed as this?

Whose clothes have I taken?

Whose eyes have I gouged?

Whose skin suit have I planted within?

Which part of me has come to find in this, myself?

Meral Alizada

The most beautiful I had ever looked,
Was the most damned I had ever been.

Meral Alizada

I come out each night,

My death on my mind,

But why is there a spanner in the works of suicide?

Plans cancelled,

They cannot open my door

Why do they show their colours?

Sinister bright

These bonds,

A mere season lifeline

There is a keeping of myself,

From myself

But what is keeping me?

Meral Alizada

This body,

Foreign second skin

As if it were not mine

As if all I touched,

All I held

Burnt and burst into my hand

Money became water

And that water precipitated

Becoming air

The air, vacuous

Boneless teeth

And empty veins

The beating heart of dreams

Stabbed purple and blue

This was a place,

Where nothing grew

Meral Alizada

An incitement of movement

A severe self convincing

Ecstasy

A forced strenuous conviction

That this is somehow, happiness

Their faces

Misted

Vomiting out all that was kept in,

Pig faces in the ultraviolet

And in this mist,

A body of no vibration

Smoke cloud consuming his face,

Moved *closer*

Meral Alizada

The whisper

The faint whimper

The gentle tapping at the window

And I would stir and rise from my sleep

A whisper

It knocked silently

On the door of the heart

In an attempt to liven

What was deadened from within.

How did what was abhorrent,

Repulsive

Become lifestyle?

It asks

How did you come to dine

With the eaters of the soul?

Meral Alizada

Why this seering pain?

Why is there drowning from within?

Why does the body cry at night?

Why does the sky peel itself from these clothes?

Why do I see imposter in the mirror?

Why is it as if something

So essential has been lost,

That it cannot be retrieved?

Meral Alizada

She would reach me the sweetest

In lung serenade

Of lime green clouds

We are in clouds

Until we are not.

In la-la land's summit

Until the plummet

Gorging and gorging,

Until it empties me out

Skeletal, I rise up again,

Marrow bone,

Ashen flesh

Meral Alizada

They have come to rid themselves,

Of themselves

An endless night, it seems

But the shrieking is timed,

The clock set for the moment

The string pulls back,

And truth takes its rightful place again

- We all meet consequence and reality in the morning, every morning.

Meral Alizada

It *whispers,*

You were discontent

That purity,

You tasted stale

The protection

The forcefield of good within

And you detonated Sina's city

And fell to Epicurus' tribes

So now

You will sit right in the middle

Of their sermons

And rituals

You will be the scapegoat

The spitroast of their feasts

Sit in the middle of the fire,

And watch yourself burn

You have known the height of

That divine protection

Now,

You will know the height of this exile

Meral Alizada

When I lost my self righteousness and self respect,
I gained the easy admission of self-entitled men
A blendable figure
Malleable and loose hanging
 The veil of modesty
That held for so long
Now at mouth cannon
I am now a common sight
And common guests wade in and out
There was no more distinction
No more fight for honourable existence
But stirred and pot cooked
I mesh and die with the crowd
That looks to lessen its burning
By another body in the fire.

Meral Alizada

My body moved in

But something lifted and stayed outside

Refused to go on

Man in black,

Your eyes betray you,

I see the bewilderment in your eyes

Why has this kind of face come here?

But I do not deserve my face

So deface me.

In all this noise, I seek to hear my liberation

Yet, why am I deafened from within?

I have become the face of all those excitements

I swore were farce and farce,

Then why does each beat burn?

Why do they cry louder

But they all hear singing?

The lights they speak,

So we must darken

We must quieten

We cannot look

We must not see

I stand in the middle
Electricity in my limbs,
Shaking off,
Shake off
Why is there a sadness
Without tears?
Why in here, do I weep?

Meral Alizada

The quickness to anger

The love for what is short and immediately gratifying

The fall from one state of soul

Towards the lowest

That was what had pushed me from my deen

The structural demonic segregations

Of this world

This constant tug of war

The battle between preservation

And jenga toppling

For what is lost

When it is found again

Has changed its form, unshaped.

I want to go to the place

Where there is no battle

For the gun is heavy

And this body craves

What other bodies

Are so filled with

This world left me twice unsatisfied

And this path

The hamster wheel

Unaware of its own shattering

Charging on

Into and resumed ceaselessness

Even this admired view,

Will one day lose its appeal

As is the human heart,

Satisfied with nothing

The more we dip into fire,

The more expanded our stomachs become.

Meral Alizada

With each sin,

Did it become easier to break hearts

To become part of this gang

To gain membership in this place,

The heart slowly hardens

The water that once rejuvenated

The feeling of refreshed from within

Now insoluble

The smell of unfamiliar skins sits on my skin

Fragmented and hazed out

The scent of the self, untraceable

And slowly the world of reason

And its most simple of treasures

Its pure pleasures

Run wine with sourness

This mirror is not mine

This body, piñata

Meral Alizada

Your shadows separated you
It held you far from them
Their shadows meshed and intertwined
And you stood in solitary
The world as it walked
Wondered, intrigued
The people of the world
Asked the world,
How could you have placed
These combinations of peoples together?

Meral Alizada

I understood then

How deeply I had fallen for her green dress,

As reality and my existence

Became more so of

Pending horror,

And not much more,

The love for the plant and herb

Removed me from myself

For I became

Nothing

Lifted and light

I knew not of the world,

It span and span,

And I felt and knew,

Nothing at all.

Meral Alizada

Why is Venice concealed from me?

It refuses to open to me, the sun and stars of its beauty

Its gold lights and its masked romance

Why does it not touch me?

The air surrounds me

Why does it refuse to baptise me?

Meral Alizada

Auroras vines

Collected over me

The moulded veil

Over the pond

And I lay

Lifeless

Underneath

Suffocation

Oxygenation

God had long since left my quarters,

And taken sleep with Him too

Meral Alizada

Relief,

I am seeking relief

For I see

In the centre of this Eastern Rome,

A Madinah

How could oil and water

Sit so close

And not touch?

These two,

Protected, untouched, a veil shrouds them,

Shroud me in this veil too

God,

I am unworthy

I reek of what you asked not of me

They walk among them

They walk among me,

But they do not mingle

I am running from them now,

Yet why do they still find me

Protect me,

Please protect me,

As you protect the people of

Ablution and timed prostration

Meral Alizada

Open my chest

Breathe your desires into the lines of my veins

Sculpt me into yourself

I want to leave myself,

And become part of your wing.

- Gaslighting shapes us with razor blades

Meral Alizada

I love you, without your giving

I love you without the turning of your head towards my eyes or my heart

I love you for your laughter

For the bounce and rise of your heel in your maddest of moments

I love you for the pleasure of seeing the majesty of your youth

I love you for what you do with the earth,

Not what you can give to me.

Meral Alizada

Every time a person enters the heart,

Therein is created an entire world

A dimension for them,

Another existence

Formed on the lining of their essence

Palaces commissioned for their anticipated arrival

But the span of the heart's surface

Has become congested now

The abandoned ruins,

And nothing built

Hope buried,

And the gravesite, full

Meral Alizada

This love became palace grounds
But I could never find you
In any of its ornate corners.

Meral Alizada

The discoveries

Of his seeding,

The repulsion

That had spread to the entire plain of the West,

Came back to sit on my face

And across the city, I came to be known

The loyal home maiden

To the brothel-keeper

Of a hundred harems.

Meral Alizada

Find me soon, soulmate

I have but one more try at love

There is a crossroad I am reaching

I don't hurt for hurting

I know the dance of calculative depletion

There is residue

Dark spots forming on the crater of the conscience

And

I am beginning to become what I never believed

Myself capable of becoming

The process is beginning,

Please come before it is the end.

Meral Alizada

I held your shoulders
Towards the arch of the sky
And danced,
As the noor soothed the broken parts of you
And you,
You smiled the entire time,
Created an empire of deception
Infiltrated into my veins,
To corrupt me,
Delivered such
Masterful betrayal
Such energy raised in you.
But you refused,
Withheld the most human decencies from me
Had this love been cast into the world,
Every drooping flower
Would raise its head,
Deserts would flood with streams,
Honey and yellow on all lips
The world would give up its arms,
And yet you could not.

Meral Alizada

I had sat in tolerance

And in stillness

Through this massacre

One more push

One more forgiveness

If you change now,

If you slip,

You are to slip and change forever,

The bridge between goodness and wrongdoing

Is but one stride across

This path is narrow

And the tightrope

Slipping and sloped

I ask you for one more act of forgiveness

Keep your little hands

Over the tea light,

You are promised your heart's desire,

It is but *one* act of tolerance away

Meral Alizada

I am filling and giving out to you.

I am sending out these vaults to you

Are you receiving?

Will you receive?

The city points me further to you

As I move closer,

I wonder if you move, too

Meral Alizada

I miss the safe space
That love holds you with
When you begin to fall
Before loving
Meant being thrown to the wolves
Before love meant anything, but love itself

Meral Alizada

My good deeds will circle you

You will not be rid of the sounds

Of my shrieking

Your life

Is adorned with the fruits of my endless labour

I watched your steps

As you walked from me,

And I counted your steps as

You walked towards me

My letters and words

The warmth of the room

That open arms welcomed you

Will become the very fire that cooks the

Stomach that dragged from me my right,

And filled yours

Parasite

You did not make me,

I made you

In this way

Allah gave us both what we wished

In this way

I will stay with you forever

You will never know a sound slumber

For you took too many of my nights from me

For if I know my God,

There is a grave price to pay for the

Soul murder of a heart dear to Him.

Meral Alizada

In the most trying of moments
When the world has turned its roar to me,
Turned my hopes to cinder
I think of you
They hurt me,
And I wonder
Of the taste of your kisses to comfort me
They overlook me
And I wonder,
How will those enigmatic eyes
Blink to my tales?
I know your mannerisms,
I know the patience you will walk
And sit with
How I will be so overcome with the
Beauty of that blinking
That I will not
Know time nor fatigue,
Nor the past or concern of the future

Meral Alizada

I look not upon my face,

But wonder,

How will you look to me

How will your chest feel cushioning mine

Crossed legs and open hair

On some rooftop baked under the sun

I will point to the parts that hurt

I will point to the graveyards of my scars

I'm going to tell you everything,

I'm going to tell my soulmate, everything

Meral Alizada

I built you up
Not so that you may meet me
But go further
When your bricks lay,
You pounded me into the very concrete
I smeared over for you.
In loving you,
Honouring and nurturing you
I saw giants in your foot soldiers
The only one to have refused
The dance of your widespread ridicule.
I looked to you,
With so much tenderness,
Forgetting that tender meat
Made for fantastic slaughter.

Meral Alizada

I catered to your every whim
As mother to a son
I left no trace of your sadness
Go unnoticed and undealt with
I did not let a single promise
Of mine to you
Go unfulfilled
There was not a second
That my attention was
Diverted from you
All of the turns of my axis,
Orbited your moon and stars
How could nothing of this,
Have moved you?

Meral Alizada

I follow your eyes,

Those wondering eyes.

And I wonder

When they will settle on me

But they never do,

They *never* do.

Meral Alizada

How your hand did not twitch
Did not shake
In setting fire to the very place
That raised you from the sewers in which
You so comfortably dwelt

Meral Alizada

I stood at the neck of those dreams

For the revival of yours

For the sake of your manhood

For your sake of knowing

What could be seen

If you moved over

To the land of the living

But your place was in

The barren wasteland

I swore could not have been you.

Meral Alizada

Both of us remained constant
I in my mercy,
And you,
In your cruelty

Meral Alizada

My home opened to you,

You soiled the path behind you

And I swept

Swallowed

My eyes moved not upwards

Those moments of youth

And the backstab upon backstab

The collected pool

Of bruised blood in my throat

Teeth full

Bend

Bent at the knees

Palm kiss

You betray in the clothes

Picked out

Rush

For you

Meral Alizada

I will never forget the strike of that

First heart break

The first piece that shattered,

And the darkness that fell for so long afterward

We made love, living hell

We settled for a love,

That was living hell

Meral Alizada

How you ran,

How you still run

With my hair and blood

At the bed of your nails

And I run in the opposite

Spilling the mother's milk from my lips

Beaten white from your horror shows

- Infidelity

Meral Alizada

Your world
Saw no mercy
Law of the jungle
Survival of the fittest
Colourful content
How I embraced this foreign place
How I held its children to my fore
How I bowed to your people,
And my bloodline
Hung its head.

Meral Alizada

Held your hand
Straightened the spine
From ape
To sapien
The voice behind the mic,
In exact tone of the exact confidence
I took from myself,
And gave to you.

Meral Alizada

Even a child winces at pain
And draws themselves in,
Refusing to touch again the cause of its bruising
What kind of death is this?
That can lay very much alive
On this bed of rose thorns
And walk for miles
Without noticing the trickles of blood
Little fountain behind the foot
And the little drops on the pavement

Meral Alizada

I watch you,

An arrogance of a new life made

From the blood and sweat of my brow

You swing around,

A gentleman in bow tie

And yet I,

I dwell in the insanity

Of the animalism

In which you dressed

The first night,

You reached my gates

Meral Alizada

I showed you the canvas of the skies of my childhood
And yet your heart could not move towards me
Before the houses that call us to God
How could your heart not have been washed
How could not one pavement slab of that place,
Have changed your stepping?

Meral Alizada

I do not grieve for you

I grieve for the elegance with which

I loved you

The immaculate loyalty

And unfaltering consistency

The extraordinary kindness

The extraordinary patience

All of which I refused to grant to myself

A love I believed I myself

Were unworthy of,

I gave you.

I grieve for the heart that has seen

That there exists people as

Horrifying as you.

I came to you

A woman who knew not of culinary art,

Who knew not of consistency to herself

Whose life was shattered

With chaos and manipulation

But came to love,

As if she had never hurt before

And served,

As if she had served her entire life

Who took your pains and swallowed them

And as you grew,

As your height moved to a thousand feet,

I fell

And you watched me,

And knew

You watched my fall from glory

You heard my screams

I pointed to the ladder beside my falling

And you refused to give that too

I watched as you took the fruits of my givings

And planted their seeds in everyone you saw and I watched

Grateful for the opportunity to give back

To a creation of God

Refusing for you to be

Anything less than

The perfection and purity

With which this

Poets' heart

Painted you with.

Meral Alizada

My constant companion

My most constant companion,
My most loyal companion
You and I,
We sit and bathe in each other
Compatible and complacent
The both of us
Unwilling to leave
Pillow stained pillow talk
I see you in everything
Everything brings you to my doorstep
You are the guest I have
All the time in the world for
You rear your head in everyone
You broke my voice
Nightingale
My words have never been so layered
You and I,
You made me
And I, your greatest fan
I do not know any other living but this
You taught me, that you will remain

When all else passes

Your hand in mine,

Your lap I recline upon

Never leave me,

Never leave me.

You took all the capacity

The electromagnetism of myself

To be loved

And you in return,

Showered me,

So showered me,

With an astounding madness with which I paint

Broken and brilliant

Mad and enterprising

It was you,

That lifted me from my bed

That catapulted me into chasing

The names

And the faces

You came in such waves,

In unspeakable volumes,

That I grew immune

To any physical discomfort

Time
Nor health,
Nor etiquette
You blinded me to all,
I knew only you,
Only you
All senses depleted,
But I could never fill myself enough
With you.

Meral Alizada

I indulge in the crumbs left

Of the love

You give to others

To revive myself

So that I may continue this loving

And pray,

That this love makes it to the morning

Meral Alizada

I move my face but little

It remembers not when it last

Pulled the apples of the cheeks from its tree

Have you ever felt such sadness,

That your lips have forgotten

The direction of a smile

A body that stood capable of it all

That bent but never broke,

Now tip toes

Trembling on warmed ice

Knowing at any point,

It can meet the tip

Meral Alizada

I tire of the sound of warplanes

And shatter glass

The burning of my thousand libraries

The soiling

The occupation

Of the springs of my gold tops

Each burst of insanity,

A reminder

Another nail in the coffin

Of a soul buried two years ago

Of the damage that was done

Of the warfare from which few recover

My mind in a constant state of doubt

How I run and run in circles

Flaring,

Burning from within

How the cool of my waters

Have turned to lava and burn black.

Happiness knows not my face,

Static stands in the spaces between

The steady and the run wild

The rise of my vibrations

Have come to choke me now

O high and pushed back shoulders

And steady legs

Your walk

Electrified the cousin mother of your roots in soil

The pull and health swell of my chest

Worn weak and thin

I am but a shadow of who I was

Coward

I cannot look to the mirror to testify

I walk in shame,

I walk in shame now

And this is my reality.

There are permanent markings to this now

While the criminal

Has but returned from sun and saffron,

With no dent in the smooth canvas

Of Kandahar's clay

I lost everything

To gain this affluence in pen and hand

A bargain to remember,

While blood still runs

Across the temple floor

Meral Alizada

The dream

The bliss that came
In the days that followed
The dream in princess gown
The sound of violins in the open chamber hall
Chandeliers,
My back filled and steadied
Held
Guarded
Each eye, rise
You were looking before I looked
So new having never known this
As if the hand of God
Stretched outwards
To steady me
A quiet promise
Between Him and I,
As I held out,
A little, just a little more

Meral Alizada

And I wondered,

Amongst those people

In one of them,

There could have been you

Still out there,

Perhaps still waiting,

But perhaps not.

An ode to the soulmate I was yet to meet

The soft mannerisms,

The rhythm to a walk only he can replicate

Those little things,

Will I know these little things?

- Released when I am from this captivity, I will find you.

Meral Alizada

And how terrible is the world.
That you can put yourself up for sacrifice
And still be told,
Your meat doesn't quite make the cut.

Meral Alizada

I watched her, green eyes and white skin

Jackpot formula

The sight of her alone was enough

Her smooth twirling

The long lashes that

Wrapped you over and around her finger

My own glimpse caught in the reflection of the grey shine windows

The bulk and average of my face

My tactless masculinity

No flow between the arches of my body

And no capacity of my hands to hold onto anything or anyone

And I realised

The facial lottery

As orchestrated by the

Turban head men of old,

Worked far faster than the true love

My plain face,

Could ever hope to give.

Meral Alizada

When you love more,

Your performance eyes stand ready for service

When you love more,

You lay awake

As they lay in deep slumber

When you love more,

You love them so much

That there is so little to love yourself with

And that can't be the love

That will be yours forever.

In loving more,

Do you lose them

For while you love them,

They find a person who loves themselves

And loves them

Only,

For their self-love

Meral Alizada

I look to the mirror
And it amuses me
How someone so small,
Could house so much pain

Meral Alizada

Your words

They are carved into the fear of meeting the mirror,

The deep bearings of your betrayal,

They sit so vividly

On my face,

That the world wept for me

While I keeled over

Refusing to believe

It had come to this

- Holding the ashes of myself, unable to pocket what is left.

Meral Alizada

We either fall,

Or we don't at all

Tipping over the ledge

And being thrown over

Gripping for life,

Is still not falling

Falling, is falling

Falling is falling in trust

Falling forever,

And knowing there is no way we can thud.

- There is no honour in unreciprocated love.

Meral Alizada

Are you every man's woman?
I had always remembered you
Always known you to be
Acquired taste.
Where did your elusiveness travel to?
What price did you pay to sell your originality
For massness?

Meral Alizada

I sit with my chest pulled open

Revealed to the heavens

These grey fingers

Reach in and scoop its ashes

Held to the face of the sky,

These skies disgrace me

The stars have turned their backs

I beg of you,

I beg of you

To Whom I have no face to beg,

Resurrect me, O Lord

Resurrect me,

Entice this soil to grow again

Holding out the folds of my gaping losses,

I am smoked up,

And out

Meral Alizada

Release me of this

Of the manipulation

The retaliation

The covert lamb skin

Why am I so surrounded by this

Decadence?

Why does my skin stick to it?

Why am I tested so?

Meral Alizada

How I ache to pick up

The pieces of myself scattered

Across the foreign halls

The strange houses

The traces spread about the town

My digital defamation

How I ache to collect them together,

To turn back

To blockade myself from

Ever reaching those damned doors

To make of myself, confetti.

Meral Alizada

We died over and over again

Over, and over, again

Our bodies chemical graveyards

And we did it all over again

For without it, we could no longer be

The people we believed we were

We no longer walk upright,

Whiskers and claws,

Having come to take their feed

Meral Alizada

Punishment by Blindness

When I did not wish to see,
Allah blinded me completely
He covered the truth from me
And on the path towards falsehood
And falseness,
All would enter
But the truth
I could not see
I could not see
And now I ache
I ache to know you,
I ache now to see
Let the heart open
For it is deadened
Let it be revived Allah
Let that first step
Towards what was meaningless
Be removed
Take me back,
So that I may cut the very limb
That stepped forward.

Meral Alizada

Mercy,

With each of your lashings,

I screamed mercy

For I cannot move from this

For this is my repentance

So let me sit in this

This story

Is etched into the stars and moon

You and I, we will stand

The world, the walls, my witness

And I will have returned,

All that I lost.

For this is His Promise

The soil and the earth,

Each ring road and pathway,

Witness

They placed into the folds of my skin

And finally, made this room a home

Meral Alizada

As your cauldron

Cooled

And you moved from this place

I could have sworn

Everything in this place took a deep breath

As the space expanded,

As all settled in this space

I turned, eyes darted to the heavens

You and I

We will have our time

On that day

Of thousands of years

You and I

There are unspeakable crimes

Untouched justice's scales

And I will not rest until they tip

Meral Alizada

I sat inwards, rigid and unnerved
And they sat as bodies of water
They looked forth
Neither left or right
And they did not walk,
No no,
They floated,
Breezed through,
In regal attire,
And shining, pleasant faces
That invited not excitement,
But peace
Faces that beckoned respect,
A smiling contentment
Focused and free limbed
Amongst the Queens,
My peasantry came to sit
Their clothes looked heavy,
But their fores, open,
Their voices milken,
Little startled or distracted them.

Yet I,

Dressed for the world,

A poster of productivity

Could barely raise my breath to speak

Coming from a thousand days that ruled me,

Amongst the directors of their own day

    - An audience with Kings and Queens

Meral Alizada

Hunched over into the corner,

Determined to sit alone,

But destiny's doors broke open

Immediate infatuation

Curls and eyes of wheat,

She held my face and

I swore I could bring to scent,

The smell of my blood in her veins

She came from nowhere

And her face,

In wake of a transformation

And all my eyes and mind,

Called to bare witness

Meral Alizada

She came to me,

And as she walked,

Did the musk from her trail rise

The eyes that kept to its purpose.

Islam had never come,

So beautifully dressed

Meral Alizada

And we sat, two girls, one dressed,

A picture of the moon,

And the other a madwoman in tousled, pulled hair,

Sharing a secret of God…

Crowding around the fire of ilm and daanish,

The fall of grey hair and lines, and the rejuvenation of two lifelines.

One several steps ahead,

The other, turning in the direction,

That leads to the first.

Meral Alizada

In a world

Where we all took shortcuts,

Side streets and backdoors,

She gracefully took on the wrath of the world

And the thousand shackles

At her ankles,

For the long way round

For uncompromised principle

The way of honesty

The way of Him

And her blessings cemented

In ways,

Our conveniences did not

Meral Alizada

Death of Haya

I watched her

Wince

At my new normal

My face rested, indifferent

To this decadence

But knew no contentment otherwise

Her face contorted at this,

Mine, remained flatline

Her world, retained a freshness,

And my world dulled to bleak blackness

For when all the limits had passed,

There was no newness

No sweetness in any fruit

Extravagance

The forced injection

The planning phase

Of a high

Higher,

More intense than the last

And the world's masturbation over novelty,

There was now only dullness

In our constant

Like men who had run a thousand lovers thin,

It became habit,

That is all this was,

Habit.

Meral Alizada

Her voice,

The only one of reason and calm,

A tone heavy in principle,

She looks to me, the eyes of a comrade,

You have known devils now

You have been their sustained target

Number one,

Most wanted

You are a good person,

Care to think the devil will leave you alone?

    - I knew then, what had been spannering my works

Meral Alizada

Under her warmth,

I looked to the mirror

And I became once again

Fullness and red cheeks ripe

My mother,

I am child

Taking my first steps before her

And her, beaming

This bond, rooting

Meral Alizada

She woke at dawn
And bowed
Her shoulders inwards
She became as tall as street lamps
And rose as giants do

Meral Alizada

You covered me,

You closed the doors,

And you covered me

And I in my love for you

In my love in pleasing you,

Moved your way,

Believing it would please you

Only to find that through you,

I was pleasing Him.

Meral Alizada

Yesterday my soulmate died

So tonight,

We perform his last rites

For had he come

He would have come

Before all these inflictions

Love does not love those

Who let themselves die

No.

Tonight,

The journey had come to an end

In whimper

Meral Alizada

Every form of love I touched

Died

I had so little,

That I held on so tightly to each little thing

Ready to give my entire self

For receiving so little

My devotion

To whom

Loyalty, is but a noun

And my heartfelt affection

Was their strangulation

And He

He had been calling me

In the missions that were dismantled

The delays,

The diversions

I cast into

With bone strength

And they slipped

But I touched your Hem

And you lifted me several dimensions

Above
That which I strayed
I moved an inch close
Declaring your wisdom
Without falter
And You illuminated
What gave me wings
To leave.

Meral Alizada

Let not one action

Be covered with a half lie

For one covering

Over the truth,

Removes the truth altogether

There are layers and layers

Under them

In these half truths,

I cannot breathe

For they are no truth at all

Allah,

Open my heart

Let me see the path back to truth

For I cannot taste or know anything less

Than the absolute truth

In honesty,

There is sight

Cover the eyes of others from the right to the truth

And Allah will surely cover your eyes from the truth of this world

Even the beauties for your contemplation

They will not know place in your hearts

All your efforts

Turned to dust,

If it does not come from the face of *sadaqat*

To the gateways of the fabric of the soul,

Cleanse

And recleanse

This temple of the self,

Must shine

Do not conceal yourself,

And Allah will not conceal from you

Unveil,

And Allah will Unveil Himself

To You.

Meral Alizada

I looked to you,

And wondered what

Must drive this

Desperate Blinder,

Horse eye

Put thyself first,

And put none before

I wondered

And I remembered

You made me remember

Before I had become

The doorstop

And impact shield

Of an overgrown child,

I did not realise

This was worship.

This was another kind of honouring

Without which

All is farce

And all love,

Sham

And no truth in truth

And no knowing

In knowledge.

- When you put yourself first, you put Him first.

Meral Alizada

In the silence,

The mind began to reach for itself

Piecing together

The kaftan

Cashmere

And the scarves

The rugs and Constantine tapestries

Released from the whisked potion

Of adrenaline and mask

The raw power of confusion

Dragged by its forelocks

Weeping, its power lost

And I clothed myself with myself

Touching, touched of myself

And serving only,

Myself

After so long,

Just,

Myself.

Meral Alizada

In the quiet that you could not bear,

In the quiet, did she,

The vibrant voice within

That you silenced,

Came to play

Another soul

Upon my soul

We fused

Protected

And in need of no other

An old part,

An ancient felt part of myself

Returned to myself

And in this space,

In my oneness

That I had so long despised,

No one could taint or dilute what I was, and am

For the touch of others had so long spoiled my own essence

Here, there was no scramble

No active battle to shield the self

Here there was only myself, being washed of myself

My world being returned to me once more.

Meral Alizada

Full tank,

My stomach empty

You give out

Depleted

Overhung

Darkened car parks

My smile

Sunken

The drops on the velvet

Moistened

Smiling

The comfort of the soft crown

Neck nuzzled,

My ears cradled

We revealed ourselves more and more

As the seasons and days lightened,

So did the truth of your face

And the truth of mine.

Meral Alizada

In between the lashings and

The breath gulps,

The drag across the floor

The muted tolerance of

The sound

Of leather beating

Against meat,

The wide eyed whimpers

Pillow smothers

The slicing and mass burial sites across my crown and scalp

Will one day,

Know kiss mounds

The lowered head,

The endured struggling,

The tears that would break,

They will feel a hand that will

Keep them from falling before

They have formed.

Your voice appears,

And I leave my body,

And I look in between his

Towering cyanide,

A kind face, but without

Features,

A voice, mellowed and

Softened

Smiling in between the

Triangular view

I am coming,
I am reaching close,
The drag of my body
The beatings to the stomach
They will become caress and
The dashes at the forehead
The launching of these heavy
Hands,
They will know your kisses
And the body that knows his scorned
Absence,
The frozen over of those merciless
Misleadings,
Will know the scent weight of your
Body
And remains when you go
And you will stay,
As if you have never left
And the animalism
The take, rip open
Usurp and feast,
Will one day,
Come in small gifts
And thoughtful exchange
The deserting and vanishing
On the days of my need

Will one day,

Know his warmth at my side

And we will never know again,

Crushed promises and taken rights,

For I will look into eyes

Who cannot give

Anything but truth

An honest tongue,

That speaks no other language

I leave this body

And its nerves clog feeling

And I travel to the edge of the

Room

Of the street and the floor,

Calling out

O my equal,

O my sanctuary

This heart holds patience

In the dreams

That beckon you

The hands at present,

That wash and walk,

They will eventually shake,

The conscience stands guard

Over the heart that cannot

Precipitate foulness
And the promise,
The comfort to the heart,
A promise that whispers,
Your day is coming
He is coming,
Your Lord will replace every one of your fires,
With water.

Meral Alizada

A dua in Istanbul

May the smiles that curl against your dimples, come, true
May you walk again with the same conviction of yourself, once more
May you rise and settle each night and each break of morn,
With the serenading passion you once ignited in the hearts of
Everyone you touched
May your daily death and inward pressuring struggle lay its head to rest.
May you stop this, so that the last remaining drop of vitality, the
Trailing shadow of youth may be preserved.

Meral Alizada

All that you inflicted

What did it do to you?

Those pieces you shaved and diced,

Where did you place them?

The mountain of your carcass

Ran tall

These streets,

Easter egg hunt

These paths

And benches,

They point to the parts of yourself

That you cut from yourself

Your reduction

And your murder

Those heartbeats,

Those strides

What came of them?

These carcass shavings

Those astounding wounds

Flesh seals

The blood pools

Buried in the back houses of this little place

They are testament to what you forsook

Meral Alizada

Section Four: In Contemplation

After all these years,

These months of trying to reel in

Warm flesh expeditions

In skeletal orbs

Did I realise,

I had some far greater business,

A far greater striving than this.

Meral Alizada

There are some blessed starred nights,

I turn

And think of a smile

A single smile

Without a face

The smile is kind

It is full

It is gentle

It embraces all parts of me

The hands are without form nor line

Yet they caress me

He stands over me

Drinking from me

And I drinking from him

How I've spent a lifetime

With my eyes blazed against the stars

Counting their beads

As if each one

Counted me closer to you

Meral Alizada

You took so much from me,

That I will take from you now.

All that you gave me,

Exactly nothing else but soul death,

Will become these words and this art.

And this art will one day,

Circle the world and hold recitations in the hearts and lips of good

Heart lovers

They will know of you, point to you, and run from you.

For my heart break will not be in vain.

This story will not go untold.

In my death and my rise,

A thousand other hearts will rise too.

Meral Alizada

I will one day be remembered
Others will gather around the fire,
I will hold others hearts and they will hold mine too,
We will come together through words
And the harps of our heart's storytelling,
And one day, I will forget that I was on my knees,
At the cheek of the ocean floor.

Meral Alizada

I looked back at that time

When everything burned

Stripped and pulled from its roots

Why was there so much conflict?

Why did I not learn?

Why do these patterns hold place in my heart?

Why did it all come to mess?

Listen now,

Your formation and your change

Your evolving is now

It is within your grasp

It is not above you

It is a right you were made capable of claiming

None of this world is above your reach

You sit atop this world,

Let it not sit atop you.

Meral Alizada

The silent inward battle

The truth is,
You can scrape the surface
And I am keeping a thousand demons
Of that time of insanity
In chains that threaten to only break
I am silent
For I am deafened by my own
Scream, internal
Yet I sit before you
Completely still

Meral Alizada

A voice of good
It broke in,
A most cherished intrusion
It broke in,
It bled
And bled into the desert plain
The place of airborne poison
It washed and washed,
Until my lair of containment
Became my greenhouse of protection

Meral Alizada

In willed exile did I see,

A soul enraged at its deflowering

Would not serve any part of me

The conscience that holds trial every night

Sleep was for the clear conscience

A gift,

Luxury

For what holds sleep hanging from above

May be the sound of the protest of your soul

So I ask of you,

Consider yourself before you transgress

Do not inflict upon yourself filth.

Muting your guiding voice,

Wades us into the wilderness

The world punishes enough,

Let it not come from your own hand

Meral Alizada

I wait for you,

I wonder of your face

Of the depth of your voice

When these words are drawn to me,

And the flesh wounds begin to throb,

I remember you

And wonder,

Whether these endless

Heartbreaks

Are the reason

For the coming of you

And for you,

I await.

Meral Alizada

You bring me hope
You give flasks to my travelling feet,
It is as if I have been put to shame through the old town
Taken through the streets
And pelted by stone throwers and their tongues lashing
But they are kind,
They are only kind,
For they are leading me closer to you

Meral Alizada

These bones that burn

And my face, crimson suffocated

Will move the way

For salvation

And I will one day find myself at Your mountain,

The rest I have felt in dreams,

I will know that rest, with You.

Meral Alizada

I turned my head from

The misted mischief

Neither man nor woman,

Neither person nor animal,

Lured me into the hounding dogs place

Detangling me from the spit roast of the salivating wolves,

You saved me from myself

Rescued me,

Celebrated me for my child steps

My Bestest Friend,

My Greatest Ally

Brought to me companions

That spoke Your words through their lips

Retained me in health and pen

For so little I came far for,

And the world, You placed at my feet

I yearned my life into sourness

For those eyes of mother and father,

But those eyes were always with me

How did I not see,

The joy, the whistled merriment,

As I came to walk, to He.

Meral Alizada

The more I kneeled

The more I bowed,

The more I cut of myself

The more I sacrificed

The more you ruled in whip

And lash over me

For this is what it means to hand

Oneself over to a human being

But there was only high rising

In those deep bows

There was only elevation

At each sajdah

Love for him

Has you cutting veins

And giving oxygen to his ego

But love for God

Will have Him Holding you

From yourself

Holding you from cutting what He

Lovingly gave to you

For in the loving of yourself

You come to love God

Meral Alizada

We were all meant to

Find the very spark that

Keeps us over the fire

To be good,

To be at peace,

One is to surrender

Oneself to God

And to occupy the space

In between the meeting of the Artist,

With making the days fruitful

To experience a bliss

One can experience in this

Existence,

One must find that passion

A purpose that is so

According to the

Holder of the Soul,

The serving of your characteristics

To create an existence

Around your passion,

That is to be happy

Here

Today

And a good today,

Makes a thousand great

Tomorrows

Meral Alizada

All of it comes round

It turns and turns

And comes all the way

Back to you.

Only you

Again and again

Every occurrence

So personalised

That you go round and round

Believing yourself to be secondary

And separated from all that meets you

And yet,

Every person,

Every concept,

Every direction

And infliction,

Every encounter

And every blessing,

Staged for us

Determined for us

In each thing, there is us

We are simply reflected

Back onto ourselves

- This is your world, and only yours.

Meral Alizada

How could I have fallen at his knees for provision of humanness

For the most basic of allowances

Stripped below survival

And yet my hands held the key

And the lock came with the door,

So consumed,

That I had forgotten,

The contained prison door,

Ached to swing free.

Meral Alizada

Long after he had gone

And the confines and shackles

Around the throat and heart of my soul

Released

I knew then

That penance was my destiny

Her justice was my suffering

My soul,

She walked to me

And held me by the collar,

Her eyes wilted with a pain

I could not bear to see

That I in all in my pains, had never seen.

She shook me

Again and again,

How could you?

How could you?

Meral Alizada

She demands to know

Why did you put me through

What was not of my world?

What was beyond my capacity to carry?

I have no answer

The trial with the self,

None more painful.

Meral Alizada

At least in that aloneness,

There was dignity and honour

At least there were admirers

And no beloveds

At least there was respect

Even if there was no affection

Perhaps what I craved

Weighed much lighter

Than what I had before me

And I,

Foolish starved child

Too concerned to be filled

With bread and water

Blinded to the glorious banquet prepared before me

My unworthiness

Tossing all of it

For something so thin.

Meral Alizada

They do not tell you

That the pain is not during the slumber of numbness,

Neither is it in the infliction upon infliction

Of self- death,

Nor in the hurl of the battleground

But in sobriety,

Does the full face of the damage

Come into the sun

Meral Alizada

You made a woman of me
You cut until I bled and bled
And as I did,
New rivers began to wash at the
Bed of my ashes
You hardened what was soft
And softened what had hardened
In inflaming me
Did you remind me
Of my place at Water's side.
And somehow,
Somehow,
In this final blow
Pulled ripe,
I am running to full bloom
Full, full bloom.

Meral Alizada

Those who crave your attention

Demand far more from you

Than they give to you

But love?

Love is self sufficient

Love is selfless

Attention is paper thin

A red lipped mistress

And love, your childhood sweetheart

Meral Alizada

Our Creator is a poet

Conducting His justice

In an endless state of love

And He chooses who to gift such a gift

With incredible precision

Such deliberate conviction

And He chose you,

Beautiful heart,

To be a woman of words

To have a voice

That can echo and penetrate

Into the stale hearts of humankind

That can soothe

And capture

Reveal and waft in

He is watching you,

Waiting to see of the Eden you will grow

With the gift He has given you

O poet soul and transparent heart,

No one is like you

No one, is like *you.*

Meral Alizada

I cannot lift my eyes

To hold yours

For everything around you,

From your conception

To your scarred existence today,

Was designed

And conspired

To harden you into

Unbelievable cruelty

To beat the empath

And pure from you

Your hands can lift

To destruct

All livelihood

Around you

Your lips can bullet

Gaping holes into the hearts of those

Who have wronged you

And yet in all your power,

In all your extraordinary capability,

You have not but lifted an eyelash

In protest or offence

I cannot lift my eyes,

Nor can I lift myself

To meet *half* of you

Meral Alizada

The lonely path to the Lord,

We begin again

This entire canvas is to be repainted

Suddenly, all is noise and disruption

And this yearning becomes melody

And this melody becomes the voice of

Him

A beauty in everything

A sanctified ecstasy

This but fair bargain

Such fair bargain

O but none of these are

Sacrifices

But liberations

Losing none,

And having gained all

Meral Alizada

All the shredded tendons

And torn muscles

Have been my hand

For seeing another but my own face,

In the mirror of knowing,

Goodness, came from Him

Punishment, from me.

　　- He does not say I will push you, but only that if you walk
　　this way, you will surely fall

Meral Alizada

Allah Revealed His Might

That night

When He sealed off my capacity

To reach back for him

When He kept me,

When He gifted me,

Exhaustion.

Exhaustion that spoke the language

Of my resistance

The only key,

That kept me from the final nail in the coffin

Meral Alizada

How I had turned this world into a ring

No fight,

Just swinging

Forgetting I had every power of who to bring into my ring

And everything that came into it, I had every strength to overpower.

Meral Alizada

You Smiled

And Waited,

Waited to tell me who you loved

And Watched me

Assigning every other name to God

But God

And in between,

You never stopped

Being my God

Meral Alizada

Prayer

Thorough and through cleansing
Of the inclined seduction of our desires
The designed deliberacy of this world
To cake us in its clouds
And in heartbeat's blink,
Are we centred
Able to breathe even in time's fearless pace
Even if surrounded by monsters of all and any capacity,
We sit in sealed protection
Remembering His Might,
So that fear of man
May be washed of us
You now tire of those declarations
Of life's brevity
That inspires you to spend away
Not cherish,
Our most priceless currency
The constant contemplation of
The quality of our actions
Physically strengthened
And emotionally soothed
To remove and to be rid of
Of what weighs
And what is unnecessary,
And what dims the vision from what

Is vital

To be in direct conversation,

And thus, in direct connection

Knowing that nothing else can touch you

But Him

Purpose,

Purpose known

Meeting the soul's Owner

Answers

Received in spearlight motion

I had always moved in a movement without purpose

Practice that did not move the innard

But only in sajdah,

Only in dua,

Did I find myself smiling, unable to hold my neck

In line with my shoulders

A dispersed, scattered mind of several thousand preoccupations and

Concerns

Becomes a constant, coherent One.

A courage of ten course meals

Nothing impossible, nothing attainable

No,

We are before the King of Kings

No one leaves with

Hands unfilled

Meral Alizada

I'll find you amongst these captivations

In the rise of my chest at the sight

Of yellow and silver ribbons across the Thames,

I'll search for you in the scent of dreams

Cascading across these monumental buildings

I'll find us in the space between two hearts poured

Over the divine of candlelight

I am seeking you out

And as I do,

This city blooms before my eyes

Meral Alizada

The world of the soul,

And the lifts of the finger,

The simultaneous softening

And strengthening of the heart,

Cupped and soothed by the Lord

Meral Alizada

And so I put down the sword

I had used to tear, slash

With passion, at my most precious parts.

And fell knee forward.

I placed a hand over my heart

And rubbed against the

Hollow of my chest

Closing my eyes,

Praying the large spikes of the mountains within,

Would smooth to rounded hills

Calm my heart,

Mend my heart.

Meral Alizada

People will break your heart
Again and again
You will know insanity again and again
Until you remove yourself
From the table of expecting
Of requiring a perfect love,
From flesh and bone
Hand yourself over to Him
This Love will not shatter you
As His Creation does.

Meral Alizada

Why have we commercialised

This ancient truth?

All the answers of which are known from within,

A placed knowledge in the heart,

So innate,

That this world seeks its distortion

For in knowing, we in mortality, become immortal

It is kept far from you, on the highest shelves,

For good reason

The heart is attached,

To the forever

And Eternal

And nothing here, is.

That is the greatest devastation

Of this life,

And the only.

One by one

All we have,

All we will be,

All who we were,

Will be lost

Mother,

Sister

Beloved,

And the self

So shed,

Shed yourself

The secret to this existence?

Let want burn,

Let want burn

For each want will be taken from you

Become indifferent to this separation

For want will hammer at peace

The soul and the spirit,

That is the only cloth to be held and worn forever

So bury the want

Boil the attachments

We will be tested

With each and every one

Meral Alizada

Section 5: Ascension

I saw my face deplete from the innocence

I so loved,

I saw myself stand on hearts

Flinch not in its crushing

The more shortcuts

And bypasses,

The lesser the nectar in the plum and cherry fruit

Less able was I to gather myself in and to my within

I saw money wilt from my hands

And success slam its doors

I did not feel as if my body was my own

My entire being shackled with several forms of insanity

The very insanity that took my sleep

My age, my wisdom and the colour from my mind and face

Reduced to a child's heart

Broken and reliant

The wrath of what it meant to chase after strangers

And backhanding the very people

Who would welcome me in any state,

I came to know that

Everything in my life,

Absolutely everything,

Had conspired to bring me back to Him

Meral Alizada

For I have found

That each prescribed act

Is in direct alignment with the seek for salvation

The certain path towards

Success of within

Soundness of the soul,

And crowned honour

There can be no more purer of a love

That we can know,

Than this.

Meral Alizada

The truth,

It came as a lump of the throat

A thudded heart transfer

All my life

The entirety of it

A mercy

A constant mercy

A mercy that washed across the canvas

Each hand movement

The provision of cellular and nuclear,

And far beyond,

Into the curtains and bridges within

We moved

By His Kindness

And permission,

Permission became kindness

For it always was.

And suddenly

But with completeness,

The counting and joining of the dots

Of how He Became to me,

How He chose for me

To have known Him in this way

In the figures across the beach

I see, Mercy

Only mercy

In the reaching of the child to the pebbles

Mercy in her arms that move across and keep her from falling

Mercy in the hold of the sky and politeness of the sea kept seated

Mercy to us, despite all we do

I had felt the smoothness of His manoeuvres

Like the child asleep

Feeling the drive

The crevices of its journey

Blinded trust to the driver

Who moves her across it.

And it was then that I knew

Why those heartbreaks tasted

Of well water and tulips

And betrayals,

Touched the soul's back with the cape of saving

Meral Alizada

I am still baffled

As to how from this place,

This barren land from which no love grew,

There could emerge

Such beings,

Such offspring

So capable

Of it

In its recognition

Its reciprocation,

And its appreciation

In a place where hand throws

Vicious and blood wounds

And tongue spit

Are schedule and survival,

From this,

There could emerge such gentleness

Therein the miracle,

Therein the Face of God Illuminates

Meral Alizada

There is greatness
In rising high enough to see
The nothingness,
The weed that cannot sprout beyond its inches
That once had witchcraft hold over you.

Meral Alizada

You are neck full in the pettiness and the bickering,

The pedantics of existence

All the while,

God awaits with want

To have you come for some conversation with Him

Putting down all other sounds, but Him.

Meral Alizada

And alas,

I will look up into the skies,

And they will not feel empty and vacant

I will feel the weight of Your presence

I will not question that You are

You are my God

And You Hold me in Mind

And Heart of all that becomes of me

The Skies that once smiled,

Are Smiling again

And I smile now, too

Meral Alizada

Hand sever the thieves of peace,

Supply cut the blood pools to the parasites

The act of mercy to oneself,

Invites the mercy of the world entire

Meral Alizada

And then it came,

The line

To love for the sake of Allah

Detached

Unattached

But connected and present

Who now gives

And leaves before expression of thanks

Let not passion,

Nor motive drive

The output of your tipping deeds

Do not be miserly or shy

In a giving that does not reduce you

A giving,

A living,

For the sake of Him

Meral Alizada

I remember the exact moment
It all came together
The reason for these digressions
For those doors that slammed,
The people that ran,
All of it conspiring
Inspiring
The only path before me,
Was His
Again and again
Everything I had done,
Ever experienced,
Ever loved and lost,
Brought me back to the Creator
To belief
To Whom
Calling yourself
A servant of,
Was to be made a warrior,
A Queen.

Look what came of you,

Trailing the streets

Disgraced,

Pitiful repulsion

And in a moment,

You were transformed

Elevated, the Queens you loved,

You are a part of them

Do not be shy to dine,

A long time coming,

But it came at last.

Meral Alizada

A veil draped across the face of the moon,

She lowers,

Her collarbone and Cupid bow

Laid at the bed of my balcony,

She holds me in maternal embrace

And whispers,

All those lives you have made fragrant,

Now it is time to plant your own garden

Meral Alizada

By dumping,

And loading onto us,

The transgressors

Smoothed the pebbles

Underneath our riverbeds

We break surface

Baby new.

Meral Alizada

How pitiful,

To have listened to

The voice

That whispered,

Taunted His way

The voice that held me in confinement,

Ruin and stifled wings

And yet,

I am more free,

Most free,

Than in the centres of that do it all,

Have it all *la la land*

In His righteous playground,

I am a child again

I am the child I lost to the free world,

Again.

Meral Alizada

How blessed is this shattering,
In fear of its shards,
I can never turn to entire lands
I cannot receive what I once did,
This body can no longer touch,
What it once *bathed* in

Meral Alizada

How each part of me
Had been watched
Parts of it mapped out
Designated instructions for
Its bombardment and ridicule
Each move calculated
For the incineration
The sterilisation of the fields of tulip,
Rose and lavender that grew in me
And yet you came,
You held my chin
The clumps of the hair
I had pulled from me
You kissed each part
Your lips
Cooling the hot coals
Joy,
Joy is filling my scalp
Baby hair rise,
They sprout out
Like daisy blooms

Meral Alizada

Live so that love may find you.

Love will tap you on the shoulder

When you are chasing your dreams

When you have understood yourself

And what is needed for you,

When you refuse to move the cornerstones of your honourable life,

It will break open the doors and inconvenience you with a light that

Will never fade

From you,

So go forth and take the world by storm and moonshine

What you desire,

Has already begun its journey towards you.

Meral Alizada

It is as if God intended to share with me,

The most tender secrets of life,

By breaking my heart while

It was still forming

Meral Alizada

We do not give this heart
Chance, reason
To be placed in a state of jousting
Or wrestling
We do not let open another door
That leads to fall without gain
For we love ourselves so,
Because we love Him most,
Why do you not submit to this inner
Voice?
It speaks of perfect knowledge of
Yourself
When has it ever come to mislead?
Listen,
Even where is mellowness
Even if there is less drumbeat
And more sound of fallwater,
Choose this voice
Let loyalty be, to this voice.

Meral Alizada

The gravity of it all

That caused each pebble to sit in these sequences

And somehow the Creator of all this was

Forever within reach

There was a way of reaching Him

A permanent unmoving unending

Inseparable connection,

That even if I pulled and tugged,

It remained constant

Unfaltering,

Knowing that He knew me

The Creator of all of this,

Knew me,

Caused me with deliberacy

To be part of this world,

To listen to me,

To love me

How could I in knowing this,

Not celebrate my every breath?

Not be grateful for my every breath?

Meral Alizada

Even in true love,

Even then,

When the love moved the scales to tip

And toe

There was friction

An outright failure of every love that spilled

Over and took the place of God,

In expecting perfection of love

From a human's fallibility,

Will render you homeless,

Heartless

He must be held at the summit of your heart,

Know your Lover,

And know Your Beloved,

Human love loves to the point

Of not running a cost to itself,

But Allah loves, with no capacity for a loss,

In loving you.

Meral Alizada

All that pain made you kind

When you wish for something
When you desire something,
You desire it with your entire being
It channels and tunnels itself into
The most kept away folded in
Places you do not whisper of,
The unrequited love
The unreturned affection,
The defeat of those loves,
Humiliation and emptiness
And yet
There is One who returns in ocean scoops
For the droplets you hand over.
O solitary building man
How many homes were knocked down
How many you built by your own hands
Of all those you stood as bride for,
How many wanted a fragment for you,
As they wanted endlessly for themselves?
Of all those sisters you were mother to,
Where are they now?
Do they remember you?

Did they frame for you a window
For the palaces you built for them?
And yet He builds palaces for you
In utterance of His remembrance.

- Come lay your bricks here, this Lover and Friend will not tear it all down.

Meral Alizada

The oasis will be found again

My skin will know

The replenishment of submersion of water

Of the Mediterranean

Of the glisten of royal blue

Turquoise

The thousand rosemary beads of hope

Will adorn my skin

The Santorini sun will rise

Each affliction onto my skin

Every twisting into

Of my stomach

The smooth petite

Little camel hump

Every blow to

My head,

The every seizure

Of my hair from my scalp,

The sun himself will bow

And turn my hair to gold thread

The wind beneath me,

Will spread my arms

The breeze

Pocketed into my spine

They will lift me

Swirls of lavender

Might blue,

This is now my place

It is within my touch

How beautiful,

That you committed this atrocity

And Allah put it back into my capable

Worthy hands to

Regain

Rise, to kneel

Your anointing

Sword of pearl

Taste the fruits of your strength

Know the nectar of the wine

The cherry and vine,

You will be anew,

As if they never,

Ever,

Laid hands on you.

Meral Alizada

I was moved for others,

Hardly for myself

As if the revelation of this secret was obstructed

By the limited seeking of the self

The constant pursuit of want

Of want,

So much want.

And none of it enough.

I understood then,

Why I had to live for something beyond myself

How I had to serve the higher stage

My self left me of me

And when I did,

The hook at my neck

Broke free.

Meral Alizada

The more I am in need of You
O Lord,
The less I need of any
And all else.

Meral Alizada

I let go
I let go of a life chasing,
I let go of the need to be loved
By a man of earth
In pursuit of a love for Him
Cementing Him into the Centre of myself
Ridding myself of all of myself, for Him,
Tongue sweetened,
And eyes washed,
My lungs filling with Him.

Meral Alizada

While my hands were cupped
In worship to You,
You filled them,
With him.

Meral Alizada

Section 6: In The Palm

The bridge cross
From the deep state of love,
To making the love
Daily practice
A life of worship
As one walks
And not a day
Without His Remembrance
The child that looked over walls
And torn veils,
Struck by their cleanliness,
By the shine of those cheeks
And fores that know meeting
With Him,
The community and the inner
Discipline
And the peace,
Oh that *peace*,
Life long mesmerisation
Somehow, came to find place
In those chambers
And made of this, an entire life.

Meral Alizada

I do not,

And I do not,

Not now or anymore,

Look to you and wish to have you,

For you cannot be had,

And I may stand beside you

I may only stand beside you,

If we live for Him in our side to side,

I can love you

Without a rope around your neck

That I tied around each love I had,

I can love you

In a way that leaves you free

And I can love you,

Without our futures held as one.

Meral Alizada

Hope will run in these veins again

The scars

Are washing with honey

The tobacco stains,

They are scrubbed squeaked clean

By His remembrance

The heart startled

Will dance in the eye of the storm

I will know myself

And that too with conviction

No one will conquer these walls

Far too many tribesmen

Their spears and their shirk

Have come to sit upon these tourmaline

Recliners

The pigs on the throne,

Under the Versailles ceilings that recoil

In the face of these foreign invasions,

Warrior rise

Your sword

In the centre of the marquee

Aches for your hands

Too many foreign hands have passed over

This silver and emerald

In seeking to meet their victories
With this
They have decapitated their own heads
No land is brother to a foreigner
No land is sister to invasion
I swear to you,
The tributaries rose
To call for their Queen each day
The pearls in the river banks
The oysters slammed shut
Awaiting,
Calling for your return
Opening to no other but you
They will reveal their paradise
To no one,
But you

Meral Alizada

Allah you soothed me, took me

From pining for person to person acceptance

Put me to my rightful place,

Never again will I live to make others comfortable,

Never again will I strive to empty myself,

In the hope of some

Backwash of the kindness

I transmit

You took from me the desire to be loved by flesh man

You took from me the constant

Fleeting

Futile, cruel endeavour to shave to hold love.

You drained my lungs of the longing for the vert desire that

destroyed me at each

Turn of my life

You took from me,

All that chained me

I am light and without form

Shroud me,

Until I am cleansed

Weather and wilt

Burn and torture the soles of my feet

So that I may reach the gates

These unworthy feet

Became a fragment of worthiness

Keep me so at level with the soil

The dark and purple of earth

So that I may never rise from my prostration

Meral Alizada

What began as a search,

A dream

To be held

In flesh arms

And loved in mortal breath,

Walked into the arms of a love

That is held and known

Without physical form,

That lives without external sustenance,

A love that can never betray,

A love of which there is no ending.

Meral Alizada

I hope that in the blemished
And congested black rubber of this world,
You can keep a rose bud of paradise
A drop of its musken scent
Safe within the pocket of your chest
A small place within
That keeps the life of goodness
Flowing in you
Concealed, but there
That little hope ticker
A little part of the heart
That you climb into caves and taverns
To gaze upon that newborn
Wrapped with the warmth of your sacred space
Her eyes as your beacon
To carry and light you, all the way through.

Meral Alizada

Do you love yourself enough,

To do good?

And do you love yourself even more,

To make good,

Your entire existence?

Meral Alizada

Liberation is in our hand

Allah is with the one who utilises his capacity

Who kisses life with gratitude

In the use of his arms and legs

In work, can Divine Miracle be seen

In striving, do we feel His Power,

That is *ibadah*,

That is belief in Him.

Meral Alizada

Had I known that those days
Would lead me to this place,
I would in singing breath,
Live each day again and again
If it meant knowing one day in
Imaan's lightspace

Meral Alizada

I hold no complaint
No demand for amends
I have no bad blood
I know no enmity
I am released of you all
And in this way I dance most free
With Him

Meral Alizada

Many learn of Him
With words and detached elocution
My entire life is testament to His Existence
My entire being, testament to His Mercy

Meral Alizada

There can be no worship
Without love

Meral Alizada

In the middle of this heart
Sits truth,
It will never love a lie.

Meral Alizada

In each battle,

Tongue's sweetness does not fade

Character, unshaken

For there is no battle

No war,

There is only defeat

And this time,

It awaits yours, alone

- To the dark troops, keep them coming

Meral Alizada

My weakness,
Love,
So I filled it with Him
Find what weakens you,
Fill it brim full,
With Him.

Meral Alizada

I took myself from his mercy

And now, I am under yours

And I slept in pain

And I woke to this garden to which you

Brought me

Your Signature

In your Creation

And You surrounded me

With the best of them

In small strides Your Way,

Do you give me all this.

How little we give You,

And how inordinately we receive

Meral Alizada

And sometimes, sometimes

I sit in this Constance

When the world dances and twirls

And the gold lights

And silk dress soirées beckon,

I do not go,

Because I know I am made for Your Marble

Meral Alizada

Be such a person that fills themselves

With such inner richness,

That the best of company,

The jewels of the world,

Come to seek you,

Long to know you,

Long to give to you,

For you know to serve Him,

So that all may serve you.

Meral Alizada

We were all children

Children bound by love

In want, in search,

And in need of love

Merely transfixed

On the dissemblance

Of its translation to us

Meral Alizada

You are crushed by this world

Devastated at what you see,

Your eyes burn and blister

At immortality, inequity

That come to cliff point of the Final Days

A rank of soul

So high and so seeking,

Then it cannot be satisfied with the paper thin pleasures

Of this mirage world

Meral Alizada

We need not music

For the within

Has begun to pluck harps

And become so melodious

That we are in song,

Wherever we go.

Meral Alizada

Every drop of good

You have let flow into the ocean of the world

Drop by drop,

Will find its way back to you

Meral Alizada

Where there is peace,

There is God

And where there is haze

And confusion,

There cannot be.

One can dance many tunes

And not understand the melody

But in truth,

There is no dancing

There is melody in this standstill,

Movement and rise in this steadiness.

Meral Alizada

You punched so many holes
And left me in the cold
Scraped hollow
Little did I know
That in walking in this forever exile
Did you give me the arms
And wings and feet
To come His way
The crowd did not blind me
Neither did the shrill and shriek
Of those bonfire nights
You kept me alone
And in aloneness
Was this knowing,
Known.

Meral Alizada

Love is of wings, do not hold it down
It is free spirited, butterfly light
And draped across you,
When your heart is turned the other way

Meral Alizada

The maddened

Insane heart

The leaping steps

The traveller's soul

Most of us bow in humility

Dare not look up

Terrified of diversion

We hold close the tick boxes of practice

And yet

There are some,

The ragged people of the dunes

Smiling as a child does

Wide eyed

Gaping at the skies

Hands of the clouds

Holding this mesmerised face

In an endless state of ecstasy

Bewildered at the beauty of the Beloved's face

The Sahara sun,

Its rays shy

They dare not scorn those enduring eyes

For they are emblazoned with a flame

Of far, far more

Meral Alizada

And I,

Forlorn seeker,

Have moved my own mind and soul

Out of the way

Crushed

Every decency

A thousand, thousand self betrayals

And yet I refused to jump ship

And in one inconvenience

We give up this relationship

Do we give up on the good

And become at loss of memory

Of all the blessings that were present

Before this inconvenience?

So why do we give up on Him so easily?

When we would not dare give up on our human loves in this way

Meral Alizada

On my hand written,

Witness and present on the first days

Of these beautiful bonds

And atop my eyes revealed,

I am meant for You

I am the holder of the greatest love story

This love has it all

This love is the only that can hold my heart

Meral Alizada

The duas you blew over every love

Dare not look twice

For fear of your own eye

In spoiling

God's preservation

Their loving,

Was as if you have loved

And been loved, too.

Did you decide then,

To keep me at Your Hem?

Did you decide then,

To give me my love and my love story

Once I had fallen in love with You?

Meral Alizada

A longing for something greater than yourself,
Is what brought you here.

Meral Alizada

Peace be upon the Soul

Who delights in the happiness of others

Who never asks to be party to the celebration

But forever hosts,

Plants and nurtures it

Meral Alizada

To the female heart who has

Placed her entire self into each love,

An eastern dream of friendship in each sister they encounter

To the female heart

Who wonders what part of itself to change or shape

To bring the desire of the heart in

It will find you,

For He Knows

He Knows the secrets whispers of your heart,

He Desires to give them You

So surround yourself with yourself

For it takes a special heart

To tolerate the dark solitude

You ask *why should I tolerate this aloneness?*

Perhaps you and Him

Must have many a deep conversation

Many dialogues,

To cement His place in your heart

Before He sets you towards the world

Like a ship of jewels out to meet the sea

So that you remember Him,

Place Him above all

Open your heart and fall,

To make you master,

And no slave of any of this place

So that victory is yours,

Protection is yours,

And the highest of heaven's honours, yours.

   - Cherish your solitude, for you are holding intimate
   conversations with your Lord

Meral Alizada

O Allah,

I do not break

Nor end

From anyone's betrayal

You have unchained me from a

Thousand chains

There is less appetite,

And more conviction

In the certainty of the perfection

And the goodness of your

Plan for me

And that You see my heart

And that You will save me

I am entrusted to You completely

And I no longer concern

Nor force the nothingness

Of my weight

Upon the scales and

Dominos

Of what you have determined for

Me

I do not interfere,

But wish well for others on their paths,

So we do not suffer on their behalf

And I am no longer heartbroken

By others diversions

Allah knows what is lethal to this heart of mine

And has promised to sustain it

And His Promise is perfection
And complete
It is He who rescued me
From the crutches of the tyrants
Of the oppressors
He revealed to me their faces
And burned out their fetish,
Scraped their taste of me
No imprint between us
And them
You will always hand me to
What is mine
You have never taken my right
From me,
For I have only taken my right
From me
I have sat witness to your miracles
I have sat at each seat
And at every angle
From the side balcony,
To the floor
It is your Theatre
And Yours, alone
Lead me,
Your Leading, is the Best Of Leads.

Meral Alizada

We cannot reach You
So we ask that You keep
At the lower heaven to touch us

Meral Alizada

The merciful face of healing

How I have missed you

This time lock has held me

In one time frame for so long,

But I ride again on the path to knowledge,

The nightingale

It knows its own song

And it sings it always

O face of healing,

And breath of courage,

He Knows how I have missed you

How I have missed the hues of You

Remembering that I too, can come to be full circle.

Meral Alizada

Did you break those relations

Did you keep me from those loves

That led me far from you,

Replaced my dependency of them

With You

So that love for You

Could have known such ease of coming?

Did you love me that much, Allah?

Do you love me that much?

That you came closest to me in my solitude

So that no one else,

Nothing else came between us

Searching and searching as child,

And You never stopped pursuing me

You never gave up on me

What ought to have been terror and dismay,

You made comfortable to me

You left me empty,

Only to be filled with you

Did you place such responsibility

Such trust in me

That even within family
I could not recline
So that I may only know recline
In Your Arms
Did you keep me from all the small
Victories of this world
So that I may know
The ultimate?
Did you give me the heart to see
The sail away
The soil over
Of all I held close
So that I may see with such clarity,
What is worth depending upon.
This home is my forever home
Made from me
And I from it.

Meral Alizada

God exists,
My survival, evidence

Meral Alizada

They are recipient to my peace
This peace moves to them
For when there was no peace
They did not receive
Energy transfer
They receive you,
Seldom your words.

- Inspire by action

Meral Alizada

Deny to your heart's content,
You and I both know the discomfort
In your throat speaks far louder

Meral Alizada

In this love there is lightness

There is trust

There is no rush nor force in this love

There is air between

For there is tawaf

Around Him

There is all handover to Him

And there is reminder of who I am

By constant remembrance of Who He Is

- When you love, with love for Him in your heart, there is a surrounding peace, regardless of what ending this story may come to.

Meral Alizada

We left it to Him

And we removed the splinters from ourselves

And we moved back to who we are

And we broke those dreams of having,

By the neck

And we put to the sea

All our longings

And we did not create lives from the loins

Of our weakened linings

We submitted to the perfection

Of His Intentions

Of His Causings

And we moved to the place of belief

And we entrusted

And we were thus trusted

And the qualities of our relationships bettered

When our greatest relationship was with Him

Fidelity in bonding

Fidelity, in His Name

Fidelity then came from all.

Meral Alizada

I thank you,

I thank you for the place you led me to

I am free of you,

In having forgiven you.

For the sake of your unbalanced soul,

I will not inflict upon this body and mind that has right over me.

For your capture by lust,

I will not cut half a lifeline and lifeforce

I thank you,

And I forgive you.

Meral Alizada

    - Forgiving him, was the final thorn I detangled myself from,
that held me from His Full Embrace

I departed from You as a child

And wept every night for having lost You,

I went on with life

But could not pass over the subtle calls

Even in the height of my sin

You sent to me

An ambassador,

Without whom none of this

Could have come together

In the gorgeousness in which it did.

Meral Alizada

How many times have you trampled

On your soul's calling?

Threw around that beautiful heart

And head of yours chasing

The limited, temporary and hollow

How you had bowed to your lover,

Left disgraced

Waning over a pain that never seemed

To go away

Betraying Him,

How could you know loyalty from anyone else?

Meral Alizada

To put Him at the Centre,

Is to never lose

A forever victorious.

We are children before Him

He Will Hold us as that,

Even if this world does not

You will never be turned away,

Abused at God's footstep

But turn up to the door of man with empty hands,

And you know the tale,

As if the tables could not,

Shall not flip

You will never crave company

For the sake of company

Your mind, heart and soul saved from the scavenging filling

Of your emptiness

You are always with Him

And He is forever, with you.

You hold your body with greater respect,

Remembering His Hand upon it

Reality is no need of escape,

You know the worth, the gift of each moment

Pains are understood

For you know what it is
And what it is not,
And most importantly, why it is
You will know the regality,
The rarity of a clear conscience
The claim back of a sleep last slept in the cradle
Everything that has been caused by this world to you,
Can be corrected by the one who created it,
Walk, my love,
He is Waiting to Run to you

Meral Alizada

Lust is exciting

It is fast faced and fickle footed

It is stagnant and selfish

No part of it makes you blossom

But love,

Love is soft

Love moves slow

Love sees all,

And refuses to go

It asks nothing of itself

But gives all,

Wants nothing

But to have some hand

In the growth and wing sprouting

That it wishes upon you.

- Lust does not meet the lovely of you. Choose love, always.

Meral Alizada

The innate justice with which you lead,

Came dressed in the perfect proportioning of your features

Meral Alizada

The pain was tunnelling,
Shaping and carving the within
Into the perfect Vessel
With which to receive Him

Meral Alizada

When you cling to God,

When you hold onto,

With all of yourself,

And weep,

No part of you reduces,

But reveal before a human,

And they will look to your

Sharp edged shattered parts

As rungs of a ladder

The airways through which

Poison can be pumped

Capitalisation of your vulnerability

The expedition to the door

Through to parts of you that cannot be replaced,

Are known, and noted.

Where is the vein that holds the supply to the rest of you?

But our Lord,

When has any part of his prescriptions

Caused to us

Distress, without inexplicable blessing?

Meral Alizada

The love for truth

Arrogance that fell heavy on the soul

And embellishment, weight and ball chain

The inward justice

And the defining compass

The love that requires no flesh touch

That would rather be without

In a sea of banquets,

The bread, the water

The milk and dates

The bare feet

The hope where it is unfathomable to be

The knowing we belong in the beyond

Sharp mind

Gentle heart

Unmoving principles

And love for the quiet

Filled with nothing

Having already, everything

Knowing eyes

Face of a child

An innate obedience

We serve, bow, only to Him.

You have come to find the perfect resting

Place

For you were, sculpted

From head to toe

The harps of your being

Finely tuned.

Inseparable and indecipherable

There is little struggle to settle in,

For this is your place.

Your perfect,

And final resting place.

Meral Alizada

We turn to the last love
With most parts sealed
Exhausted we reach
But no longer stretch.
An eye to the door
Always to the possibility of this door knowing
Their hand
We live with and without

Meral Alizada

I have crossed the seeking

For the Unimaginable Realm

I seek You.

I am in need

I am seeking You

Give me not

Rivers of this

Mounds of that

Nomad heart,

Linen lungs,

I seek you,

I seek only, You

- We have come to this.

Meral Alizada

Your place awaits
Rugged dhervish,
Welcome home.
Your bloodied soles,
Would have always found this way.

Meral Alizada

We are in awe,
In awe of what comes,
And what does not.
And we are intact
Come, what may.

Meral Alizada

I climb atop this Palm,
I lay in this Centre
I am with the Balanced
I am with the Coherent,
I am with the True.

Meral Alizada

- ENDS -